WILDERNESS WANDERIN'

ROCKY MOUNTAIN SAINT BOOK 3

B.N. RUNDELL

Wilderness Wanderin'
(Rocky Mountain Saint Book 3)
B.N. Rundell

Paperback Edition

Wolfpack Publishing
6032 Wheat Penny Avenue
Las Vegas, NV 89122

ISBN: 978-1-64119-250-7

DEDICATION

Time. The Bible says threescore and ten, that's seventy years. I've passed that mark and because of that, I've gained a new appreciation of time. When you're living on borrowed time, so to speak, it becomes more precious. And as such, I appreciate it more. And what I've grown to appreciate, is the time readers give of themselves to curl up and wrap themselves in the words written by another and let the hours tick by as they delve into the black and white imagination of someone who might be a total stranger. So, for you that so generously give of your time to read these pages, I say Thank you. And I dedicate each and every page to you, who make it all worthwhile. Thank you for your time, you really are appreciated!

CHAPTER ONE
YELLOWSTONE

HE LEANED HIS FOREARMS ON THE RAIL OVERLOOKING THE BOW spray of the steamboat *Yellowstone*. The slight breeze carried the mist of splashing water into his face and he squinted his eyes, but kept his face into the wind, enjoying the refreshing dousing. He stood erect, keeping his hands on the rail but lifting his face from the spray, and watched the trees on the riverbanks march slowly by, and the debris from an earlier rain upstream bob along with the current. One tangle of uprooted trees carried the carcass of a buffalo, now soggy and limp with its nose in the water, as it rode the waves that occasionally white-capped. The mass of flood carried rubble passed well away from the chugging freighter.

Several years and many voyages from its maiden trek up the mighty Missouri, the seasoned vessel and crew had made this a pleasant voyage for the first-time passenger, Tate Saint. He spent much of his time at the rail at the bow of the boat, eagerly searching the banks and the distances for new sights to store in his mind and heart. Every new panorama, every new vista, every new experience was treasured as he lived each day, not just for himself, but for the memory of his father. Together, they had often dreamed of exploring the far-off mountains and after his father's death, Tatum Saint Michaels, now known as Tate Saint, or by his Indian name, Longbow, had begun living the dream with his first trip to the Rockies, more than three years ago.

He moved slowly along the rail, eyes taking in everything, but he was reminiscing about the events of the past few years. He had helped some folks on a wagon train, fought the dreaded smallpox with the Comanche, befriended a brother and sister that were runaway slaves and helped them to make their way to freedom and California, and made a trip back to St. Louis. He chuckled to himself as he remembered the reason for the St. Louis trip. At the advice of Kit Carson, he chose a cabin site near a granite overhang that sheltered the opening to a cavern in the Sangre de Cristo mountains, but when he explored the cavern during some of the boring days of winter, he discovered it was an old mine that had been excavated by the Spaniards with the slave labor of Indians. After a hard day's work of chipping his way through an ancient plank door, he found the remains of several Spaniards, armor and all, and a stash of their gold bars, each one weighing over eight pounds. He had known, under the tutelage of his schoolteacher father, about the forays of the Spaniards into the south west starting with the gold seeking priest Fray de la Cruz and later, Juan Archuleta in 1664, but never expected to find the remnants of one of those expeditions.

He made the trip to St. Louis with William Bent on Bent's his usual early spring buying trip to stock his trading post on the Sante Fe Trail. Tate had deposited the gold, converting some to coin, and resupplied for the trip up the Missouri aboard the steamboat *Yellowstone* and his planned exploration of the Rocky Mountains and the uncharted territories. Tate was always the student and had savored his times of listening to the experienced trappers, hunters, and voyageurs that were on the steamboat. A better listener than a talker, he hung on every word of the veteran mountain men, although most of those aboard were new recruits of the American Fur company, the old-timers were easy to distinguish, and Tate was as easily recognized by his buckskin attire. His were not recently made and unsoiled but showed the use and the times of wiping greasy hands to aid in the water-shedding and the stains of blood showed the times spent over downed game or even blooded enemies. One old-timer remarked, "I ain't never seen bead work like you got on that thar tunic, whar's that from?"

"This was done by an Osage woman, close friend of mine's mother," answered Tate, as he fingered the beadwork at his shoulder.

"Osage? Ain't seen none o' them out'cheres, where'bouts they be?" asked the old-timer known as Knuckles.

"They're down south a mite, a bit east o' the Kiowa. Good people, big too. Most o' their menfolk are well oe'r six feet," explained Tate, easily falling into the jargon of the mountain men.

"Kiowa, ain't they friends with the Cheyenne?"

"B'lieve so, don't like the Comanch' much tho'," replied Tate.

"Wal, where we're headed, ain't many worse'n the Blackfeet, or as sum'd call's 'em, Bug's Boys. But them Crow ain't too friendly nohow, but them Assinboine'll trade wit'cha."

"Been out here long?" queried Tate.

"Come out wit' Jedediah Smith and Jim Beckwourth, run wit' Bridger oncet too, that'd be goin' on ten year ago, now, I reckon," rambled Knuckles, his eyes going glassy with the remembrance. He looked at Tate, lowered his voice a touch and asked, "You signed on with this hyar outfit, are ye?"

"No, I'm on my own, just wanna see the mountains, y'know, up close an' personal."

The old-timer cocked his head to the side as he looked up at the tall young man with a clean-shaven face, light brown hair that tickled his collar, clear eyes that showed no malice, and a frame that told of well-used muscles. He sported a Bowie knife in a sheath at his back, a metal-bladed tomahawk that showed Indian markings, and a Paterson Colt pistol in a holster on his left hip. Beaded moccasins told of his experience in the woods, and the weathered buckskins showed his trials.

"Been aroun' a few Injuns, have ye?"

"A few," answered Tate without elaboration, although he had many tales he could tell of time with the Osage, Kiowa, Comanche, Caputa Ute and Jicarilla Apache. Well versed in sign language and a working knowledge of Comanche, he could communicate with many different tribes and was well respected by most. But the country ahead, held promise of new adventures and new acquaintances.

"My handle with the Assiniboine is Big Fist," said Knuckles as he held his large knuckled fist up for Tate to see, "you got a Injun name?"

"Longbow," answered Tate simply, as he stepped back to the rail, looking at the wide streak of muddy water that pushed away from the far shore. He knew this was the result of considerable rainfall well upstream that flooded the creek-beds and ravines, bringing all the accumulated silt and debris to be emptied into Big Muddy. He knew the old-timer was looking at him, wondering about this young man and what brought him West, but the unwritten way of the mountain man prevented asking too many questions of a man's background. Tate looked over his shoulder at the old-timer, still seated among the piles of freight, nodded his head and started back to the bow of the boat.

Tate met many of the men during the voyage and talked with several when the boat made stops for wood. The many engagés, (French employees of the fur company) and most others helped with the gathering and loading of wood. Because the steamboat burned ten cords of wood a day, the stops were frequent, and the more help made them as brief as possible. Tate's gear was stacked near the stalls for the horses, three of which were his. He purchased them from a prominent breeder of the Morgan horses outside of St. Louis. The grulla gelding with dark markings on his legs and mane and a coat of blue/grey, he called Shady. The bay and black were geldings and would be used as packhorses, although both were broken under saddle. All were well muscled, powerful appearing horses that showed intelligence and good disposition, and he was certain they would serve him well in the mountains. He was pleased with the horses and anxious to put them on the trail.

It had been a long voyage, the captain said it was close to 1,800 miles from St. Louis to Fort Union, and they were now within two days of the Fort, and it couldn't be too soon for Tate. The only place he truly felt at home was in the pine trees on the side of a mountain, and he was longing to fill his lungs with the fresh mountain air and the scent of pines. He leaned forward on the rail, watched a pair of mule deer scamper up the bank and away from this black smoke belching monster on the water. He grinned at the big ears of the muleys as they bounded away to the sage-brush flats that stretched away from the river.

CHAPTER TWO
CROSSING

THE BIG BOAT NOSED INTO THE GRASSY BANK ALLOWING THE crewman to tie off with the bow lines. The captain allowed the current of the Missouri to push the now idle *Yellowstone* alongside the bank enabling the stern lines to be tied off. The boat at 130 feet long and 19 feet wide, was an imposing figure as the slow-moving current of the Missouri rocked the white monster tied to the bank. The crew was busy with lowering the gangplank and readying the cargo to be unloaded. First off were the horses, led by Tate with his three already geared up, and followed by the several pack mules owned by the fur company. The crew, along with several workers from the fort, began packing the crates down the plank. The captain had told Tate of the cargo, that amazed the young man; trade goods of blankets, mirrors, knives, combs, hoes, buttons, beads, tomahawks, axes, vermillion and verdigris, and clay pipes. Along with the usual load of 10,000 pounds of gunpowder and 20,000 pounds of lead and 12,000 pounds of tobacco. Other staples like flour, cornmeal, sugar, beans and more were among the first crates to be unloaded. In the early 1830's, the beaver market began to fade with the Easterners preferring silk hats, and the bulk of the business of the American Fur Company was now buffalo robes and other furs to be processed by the Choteau Company in St. Louis. Most of these robes and furs were taken in trade from the Indians, but Tate heard several of the men on board talking about hunting buffalo for the hides. Mules were needed for packing the heavy pelts from the mountains and the Indian encampments, but Tate noticed Knuckles separating one of the mules from the herd. The old-timer led the big bay mule toward Tate, now standing on the grassy flat near the boat with his horses as he checked their riggings.

"Wal, younker, here she be! The best paht'nuh I'se e'er had. Meet Molly, muh fine mule!" bragged Knuckles as he watched Tate for his response.

Tate grinned at the old-timer, dropped Shady's reins to ground tie him, and walked to the big mule with soft eyes. He stretched out his hand to rub the face and behind the ears of the big jenny, and looked at Knuckles, "She's a big 'un, alright. Guess she has to be to pack that," motioning to the mountain man's pot belly, "very far."

"Hey, hey, now, ya' don't need to be insultin' now, it took me some time to develop this fine figger," responded Knuckles, rubbing his belly with his palm and grinning.

"Wal, leastwise, ya got 'nuff so it won't hurt'cha to miss a meal or two," chuckled Tate.

"If'n you be through wit' yore disparaging remarks, think we oughter be hittin' the trail?" replied the old mountain man.

The two men, after many talks and swapping of tales, had agreed to travel together to the headwaters of the *Yellowstone*. Tate wanted the time to learn as much as the mountain man could share, and the old-timer wanted another summer in the high lonesome.

"Anything you need from up there?" asked Tate, motioning to the bastions of Fort Union that towered above the riverbank.

"Ain't nuthin' they got whut I want or need!" declared the old man as he did a slight hop to gain the stirrup of the saddle, and swung a leg over the rump of the patient mule.

As Tate mounted his grulla, Knuckles said, "Might wanna go upstream a mite, little better crossin' yonder ways."

"Yeah, that's a mite deep there," replied Tate as he nodded toward the river. "You lead out," he directed to Knuckles. The old-timer nodded his head as he clucked to the mule, encouraging her with, "Le's go Mabel, show the younker how we do it up'chere in the mountains."

"I thought you said her name was Molly!" called Tate from behind.

"Tis, but when I call her 'nother name, she gits a mite jealous and tries harder to please!"

Tate shook his head in wonder at the man and his mule. *This is gonna be an interestin' trip, I reckon,* he mused as he dug heels into the ribs of the grulla, following close behind Knuckles and his mule, whatever her name was.

Fort Union sat just west of the confluence of the Missouri and Yellowstone rivers, upstream on the Missouri about a mile, but the backwater from the confluence added to the depth, making the maneuvering of the boats easier, but crossing on horseback more difficult.

Knuckles led them a little less than a mile upstream to a wide crossing made easier by a wide sandy island in the middle of the river that spanned about half the distance. He led off near the downstream point of the island and easily crossed the narrow stretch that was no more than stirrup deep. His mule walked up the sandy strip, shook the water from its belly with a big roll that almost unseated the surprised Knuckles, and turned her head around to watch the followers make their way across. As Tate's grulla stepped from the water, Knuckles gigged the mule into the wider but swifter stretch. Within a few steps, the mule dropped into the deeper water, and began to bob with the current. Knuckles slipped off on the downstream side, held tight to the saddle strings with his left hand, holding his Hawken and powder horn with the other hand high overhead and clear of the water.

Tate followed the example of his adopted mentor, slipping off the saddle and holding his Hawken and horn high and dry. He had wrapped his Colt in oilcloth and stuck it in the pommel before they left shore and thought it would be well-kept there. The two pack horses stretched to the length of their lead ropes, tethered to the saddle of the grulla, but easily followed the lead gelding across. Within a couple of minutes, all were aground, animals shaking excess water causing Tate to check the rigging on the panniers and parfleches. Everything was well secured, and Tate swung aboard to catch up with the long-legged mule. As he reined up alongside Knuckles, the old-timer said, "We'll foller the north side o' the Yellerstone, good cover an' easy goin' an' them Crows usually stay on that side," motioning with a nod of his head to the far bank.

"But didn't you say, this side is Blackfeet country?" asked Tate, looking around for any sign of others.

"Wal, younker, just 'bout anywheres a white man puts a foot down is some brand o' Injun territory. All this," waving his arm around, "belonged to the red man long 'fore any o' us white men showed up. An' no matter what'chu think, don't none o' 'em like us bein' chere."

Tate stood in his stirrups to look around. The river had carved a wide flat valley that held well-watered grassy meadows and considerable greenery along the banks. cottonwood, alder, larch, ash and willows clung to the banks and the edges of the fields. Snowberry bushes fought with chokecherry for the greener stretches while farther from the stream grew rabbit brush, sagewort and a wide variety of cactus. Foothills were bunched together, split by gouged ravines and gullies, as they sat back away from the river. The hillsides were dotted with juniper, often in clusters, and bunches of sagebrush. It was all familiar to Tate, little difference from the flatlands to the east of the Sangre de Cristo mountains where he spent his first years in the mountains.

While Tate took in the surroundings, he was startled when Knuckles brought the mule to a sudden stop, snatched his Hawken from the scabbard and in one smooth motion, brought the weapon to his shoulder, set the trigger, and squeezed off a shot. Tate looked toward the tree-line beside the river and saw a young button buck mule deer drop with a quick kick and lay still. Tate was amazed to see the mule just move his big ears as if fanning away a bug, but made no other move, apparently used to Knuckles shooting while still seated. Knuckles turned, grinning, and explained, "I've been wantin' some fresh venison steak e'er since I left'chere. My mouth's already waterin', what say?"

Tate glanced at the western horizon where the sun seemed to be resting, turned back to his friend and said, "Sure!"

While Knuckles dressed the deer, Tate stripped the animals and tethered them for a graze on the late spring grass. Tate started a fire, cut some willow withes and speared the fresh cut steaks to hang them over the flames, sat a coffee pot with water on a flat rock near the coals and whipped up a batch of cornbread to fry in the skillet. Knuckles walked back from the river's edge, wiping his fresh-washed hands and arms on his britches, and sniffed the air and said, "That's what I been missin', campfire cookin' wit' fresh deer steak, cornbread, an' coffee. Musta done died an' went ta' Heabin'!"

Tate leaned back with his elbows against the log and grinned at his friend, answering, "I'm purty sure Heaven's considerably better than this, but I been missin' this too."

After their wilderness feast, the men sat with steaming coffee and looking into the fire as twilight dimmed, and shadows lengthened. Tate looked at the darkening sky, noting a few early rising stars peeking through the indigo blanket, and said, "We didn't make it too far today, but tonight's showin' some promise."

"So, you really meant it 'bout travelin' at night? Don'tchu know night times fer sleepin'?"

"The moon's waxing towards full, it's lookin' to be a clear night, an' while them Crow an' Blackfeet're sleepin', we can make some time. Didn't you say that it's nigh unto a month 'fore we make it to the mountains?"

"There ya go, naggin' at me like a ol' squaw already. Alright, alright, I'm just as anxious to get to the tall timber as you are, can I finish my coffee first?"

Tate grinned at the old-timer's attempt at showing a cantankerous nature, but he added, "'Sides, if you ain't done much travelin' at night, you're in for a new experience. Those are kinda hard to come by at your advanced age, ain't they?"

"Lissen' you young whippersnapper, I ain't near as old as you're tryin' ta' make me out ta' be! I can prob'ly whip you and two or three more like you!"

Tate chuckled as he rose and started for the horses. He threw the dregs of his coffee at the fire as he walked by and dropped a hand to the old man's shoulder. He lifted his eyes, saw the glow of the moon rising, and smiled in his anticipation to put a few miles of flatland behind him. Something was drawing him onward, and it wasn't just the appeal of the mountains. There was something, something urgent that seemed to be pulling him, but he couldn't for the life of him understand what it was, butExperience had taught him to be patient and observant and it would soon reveal itself.

CHAPTER THREE
BUFFALO

The first stars of the night hung tantalizingly low below the canopy of indigo, tempting Tate to stand in his stirrups to see if he could reach up and touch the elusive lanterns of the night. He laughed at himself for such a ridiculous thought but smiled at the remembrance of his first night under the mountain sky. He had sat his horse for the longest time, just scanning the heavens, identifying the constellations as taught him by his father. It was a special memory, because it brought his father back to his side, remembering the times they sat together in the dark near their home in Missouri. One special time was when they were grieving the loss of his mother, a woman that always helped those in need and had lost her life serving the nearby Osage village that had been stricken with smallpox. His father had talked about the doorway to Heaven, knowing his beloved wife had been welcomed home by her Savior. When Tate asked his father, "But how can we be sure she's up there," pointing his hand to the stars, "in Heaven, I mean?"

"Because the Bible tells us that 'with the heart man believeth unto righteousness: and with the mouth confession is made unto salvation. For whosoever shall call upon the name of the Lord shall be saved.' And your mother did just that. She believed with all her heart and took God at His word and prayed and asked Jesus to be her savior. Because of that, we know she is in Heaven with Jesus even now."

That simple conversation had given Tate a special comfort that he didn't understand, but accepted, and now knowing his father believed the same, he knew his father was also in Heaven. He lifted his eyes to the wondrous display of God's handiwork and smiled contentedly at the thought of his parents being together. With the North Star just off his right shoulder and slightly behind, he knew they were heading west south-west. The moon, close to full, was behind them and serving as a lantern for their trail. Tate stood in his stirrups, sucked in a deep breath, letting it out slowly as he surveyed the area around him. He could smell the mud from the river, the sage from the flats, the sweat of the horses, the leather of the saddles and gear, and a musky smell he remembered as buffalo. A coyote lifted his yip-yip mating call to the soft breeze of the night only to be answered by the long howl of a wolf. He turned to look back at Knuckles, whose whiskery face was in the shadow of his floppy felt hat, but heard his voice just above a whisper, "them's buffler," and he let a low cackle escape.

Tate reined up and waited for the old-timer to come alongside. They spoke quietly with Knuckles saying, "Guess ol' lobo done told that skinny little whippersnapper who's the bull o' the woods! That's what happens when a scrawny coyote sasses his elders. That ol' wolf'd chomp him right in two if'n they started scrappin'. An' if'n we di'nt already have 'nuff meat, I'd go fer a slice o' buffler liver."

"I reckon they're still a far piece ahead of us, but I know what you mean. Course, it ain't like these are the only buffalo in this country," surmised Tate. "We've come a pretty good way, 'fore dawn we should make maybe another ten miles or so, reckon?"

Knuckles looked at the moon, now just past the high point overhead, "prob'ly. It's just past midnight, we got 'nother four, five hours 'fore sunup. Them buffler ain't movin' much, but they's prob'ly five 'er more miles yonder," lifting his arm to the west. "Don't reckon they'll get too fer from the water, 'course the Musselshell runs parallel the Yellerstone down yonder, but that's quite a ways yet. Most o' the feeder cricks come from them hills to the South," he proclaimed with a nod of his head to beyond the river.

A great horned owl called its question into the darkness as the duo passed by with the only the occasional scuff or the click of hoof on a rock. The creak of the leather was muted by the slight breeze blowing from the river. The whisper of their moving through the grasses gave warning to the rodents of the fields and the thump thump of escaping snow-shoe rabbits was intermittent. The men traveled side-by-side, each one trailing a pack horse behind, and both enjoying the quiet of the night. Knuckles interrupted the stillness with a whisper, "I thot you was crazy wantin' to travel at night, but tain't bad, no sirree, tain't!" Knuckles saw the moonlit grin of his partner, and his chuckle split his whiskers. The moon was now before them, slowly making its way to the distant mountains to once again tuck itself in and yield the canopy of darkness to the coming sun.

Most of the stars had snuffed their lights when the grey light in the east announced the arrival of old Sol. Knuckles picked a comfortable spot with a good cover of tall cotton-woods and thick alders near the riverbank. The two busied themselves making their camp. The old-timer picketed the animals within reach of water and graze, stacked the packs close to the fire ring while Tate busied himself preparing the fire and readying the coffee. They kept near the trees where the rising smoke would be dissipated by the leafy branches. Choosing the dry, dead wood for minimal smoke, Tate soon had the fire going and coffee perking. He skewered slices of the venison, hanging them over the flames, and pushed the frying pan with cornpone nearer the fire.

"Cain't you cook nuthin' else but cornpone n' steaks?" asked the mischievous Knuckles.

"Cain't you cook anything?" replied Tate.

"Hummph! I'll show you soon 'nuff, younker. Just don't burn muh steak. If it ain't still red on the inside, it ain't wuth chewin'!"

"Why you ol' skinflint, you ain't got but two teeth to chew with anyway!" answered Tate, chuckling at the grinning old man.

Knuckles stomped away to roll out their bedrolls and check on the horses. Within moments, he returned and sat on the log, poured himself a cup of steaming java, sipped noisily at the brew, sat back and proclaimed, "Now, this is livin'!"

Tate grinned at the old-timer as he handed him a tin plate with a steak and cornpone, which the man accepted greedily and sat up to dig in.Tate said, "Hold on there, Knuckles," and bowed his head as he prayed aloud giving thanks to the Lord for the food and the many other blessings. When he said, "Amen" they were startled by a volley of rifle fire farther up the valley.

"Buffler hunters!" declared Knuckles. "But cain't tell if'n they's white or Injun."

Both men sat still, listening, knowing the sounds of gunfire were some distance away and bode no ill for them, at least at present. They returned to their meal, listening to the sporadic and dwindling gunfire, each one speculating about who and what was involved. Knuckles said, "I'ma thinkin' it's white men, buffler hunters after skins. Too much shootin' fer

Injuns. Only a few Injuns have rifles, most o' their killin's done wit' bows an' arrers," he mused as they finished their meal. He stood, taking the tin plates and pans to the sandbar at river's edge to clean up. When he returned, he stopped and listened, noting the silence. "Must be done wit' their killin' and workin' on skinnin'. Hope there ain't no Blackfeet nor Crow what heard 'em, might not be too healthy fer 'em if'n they did. Neither o' them bunch o' redskins take kindly to white men killin' an' wastin' the buffler. Cain't say's I blame 'em none, nohow."

Tate looked up at his friend, startled at what he'd heard and asked, "Wastin'? What'chu mean, wastin'?"

"Why, younker, them hide hunters ain't interested in nuthin' but the hides. Oh, I'm sure they take some o' the meat, but mostly, they's just takin' the hides, leavin' the rest to go to waste!"

Tate sat dumbfounded as he pictured the herd of buffalo, decimated by the rifle fire that filled the morning hours, and the images of skinned carcasses of the majestic beasts littering the hillside. He looked at Knuckles and said, "That ain't right! I've been on buffalo hunts with Indians and I've seen 'em when the women butcher 'em. They use everything, guts, tendons, bones, meat, hides, everything! After them women git done with a carcass, the only thing left behind is blood and offal that'sonly fit for the wolves, coyotes and buzzards."

Knuckles blustered with, "Wal, many o' them hunters was beaver trappers 'fore that. When the market fell outta beaver pelts, they had to make a livin' somehow, so I'ma guessin' they didn't think anymore o' leavin' a buffler carcass than they did o' leavin' a beaver carcass. 'course the Injuns don't see it thataway and I'ma thinkin' there's gonna be lots a' problems on accounta that."

Tate became a little pensive as he considered the selfish

disregard of the buffalo hunters and when Knuckles suggested they turn in for their day of rest, he gave no argument. Knuckles made a last look-around, checking on the horses and his mule, ensuring the remains of the fire would not give off any smoke, and walked to his bedroll, well back in the thicker alders but still near the horses for their watchfulness and warnings.

THE HOT SUN of the afternoon brought a stifling heat to the campsite and the restless men, both of whom rolled from their blankets, ready for some coffee and food. They would take their time, waiting at least till twilight before starting on the trail. As the sun bid its goodbye with a splendid display of colors, the men were rigging the packhorses and readying to resume their journey.

The moon, now full, was at its zenith when Tate and Knuckles came into view of the slaughter of the buffalo hunters. The men's camp was on the lee side of a bluff about a half mile from the river and their campfires were like beacon's in the night for anyone wanting to locate the perpetrators of the carnage. Tate and Knuckles sat their mounts on a slight knoll that overlooked the wide basin that had been the graze of the massive herd. It was not uncommon for a herd of the big woolies to number in the thousands, but the carcasses that still lay in the moonlight only numbered over one hundred. Knuckles said, "Probably only six or seven shooters, mebbe a couple extry skinners, it'd take most o' the day fer that many shooters to down that many buffler. Even then, their rifles'd be red hot by the end o' the day. Couldn't load a hot barrel else'n the powder'd blow up in their face. Some o' 'em probably had a couple rifles."

Tate surveyed the massacre, noting some of the carcasses still had hides intact and would be tended to next daylight.

He looked to Knuckles and asked, "Where they gonna take the hides? Fort Union?"

"Nah, they's another Amer'can Fur Comp'ny fort upstream a ways. Fort Van Buren, near the mouth o' the Tongue river, across the Yellerstone. They'll take the hides there, an' go after more. Them fellers could take, oh, mebbe a thousand hides o'er the summer, mebbe more. And at two to five dollars a hide, they're makin' good money. And they ain'ta wadin' in ice water to do it, neither. Some're e'en sayin' the price will go up."

Tate dropped his head, dug his heels into the grulla's ribs and rode down the slope to put the bloody scene behind him. Knuckles followed, both men ruminating on the slaughter and the men responsible. There was nothing to stop men like that, no law against what they were doing, and most would think it no different than any other occupation, but when buffalo hunters came to town to market the hides, they carried the stench of death with them and most would turn away or avoid their presence altogether. But here in the wilderness, there would be no one to stop them, except the Blackfeet or Crow that would defend the animals that were their very lifeline and sustenance for their way of life.

The sunrise painted the landscape with a glow of orange as Tate and Knuckles made their camp in the cottonwood at the river's edge. Knuckles fried up some salt pork, using the hot grease to sop up with the hardtack, making a quick meal so they could turn in and get ample rest before the hot sun of the afternoon shortened their stay. But even then, the restless men were easily awakened by the sound of gunfire coming from the direction of the hunter's camp. Knuckles sat up, listened a while and looked to Tate and said, "They ain't takin' buffler, that there's a Injun fight. I'm bettin' the Blackfeet're lookin' fer scalps!"

Tate listened to the sporadic gunfire, looked to Knuckles and asked, "Don't that sound like it's gettin' closer?"

Knuckles looked at his young friend, turned his head in the direction of the racketing battle and turned back to Tate, "I think you're right, boy. Mebbe we best be packin' up, just in case." He struggled to his knees and began rolling the bedding, as Tate stood to fetch the animals. Within moments, the men were ready for travel, but both went to the edge of the clearing to look back along the trail for any sign of approaching danger. The gunfire continued to increase in volume, but diminish in severity. Tate said, "Sounds like the fight's lessening, maybe they fought 'em off."

"Or they been killed off."

The gunfire fell silent and no other sound carried to the travelers. Knuckles said, "I shore am curious, how 'bouts we leave the pack horses and sneak back to see what happened?"

Tate looked around at the waiting animals, nodded his head in agreement, and went to loosen the cinches on the packs just enough for the comfort of the horses, leaving them tight enough to retain the packs. He swung aboard the grulla and followed Knuckles along the tree-line to investigate the source of the gunfire.

The scene they found was what they both expected. The bodies of the hunters had been stripped, scalped and mutilated beyond recognition. Nothing had been left behind except the carcasses of the men. Examining the tracks, Knuckles pronounced, "They took the wagon with the hides, all the horses and guns. Even retrieved their arrers'."

"We gonna bury 'em?" asked Tate.

"Nope. Don't really want them Blackfeet knowin' we was here. 'sides, these men are past carin'. We'll stop by the fort an' let 'em know what happened." As he looked around, he let a chuckle slip past his whiskers and looked to his friend,

"Funny thing, them hides'll still end up at the fort. Them Blackfeet'll trade 'em off just like they was their own."

Tate stepped back aboard the grulla, reined him around and started back to their camp and the packhorses. There was no reason to look back, the image was forever branded on his mind as a lesson of selfishness. These men had let their greed overlook the need of the Indians, a people that had been here long before the coming of the white man. And instead of choosing to live in harmony with the people and the land, they sought to take life without regard or regret and they paid with their own lives. This was a harsh land and Tate was learning to live with it, not fight it.

CHAPTER FOUR
CROW

FORT VAN BUREN SAT ON A SLIGHT BLUFF OVERLOOKING THE south bank of the Yellowstone River. Built of cottonwood, the palisades were rough, and the single bastion looked somewhat precarious, leaning over the walls at an awkward angle. Several tipis were clustered on the south side of the fort, apparently Crow gathered for a time of trading and bickering. Tate noticed Knuckles eyeballing the Indian encampment, looking from the corner of his eye over his shoulder. He quickly moved his mule into the compound and slipped down to deliver his message to the bourgeois. Tate tied off the horses and Knuckles's mule, and walked into the trader's store to have a look around. His retail foray was interrupted by an anxious Knuckles who grabbed his elbow and said, "C'mon boy, we need ta' get back on the trail!"

Tate, surprised at Knuckles urgency, asked, "What are you so fired up about?"

"Just never-you-mind, but we gots to get a move on, c'mon now," he pleaded as he stood in the doorway, motioning to his friend.

Tate followed him out and both men quickly stopped

when a voice from the side called, "Big Fist!" A broad-chested Crow warrior stood with a lance in his hand, unthreatening, but stoic of expression, waiting for Knuckles to acknowledge his greeting.

The old-timer turned, forced a grin and lifted his hand shoulder high and responded, "Wal, how-do Holds the Enemy! I never 'spected ta see you'chere. I take it you an' your'n are camped out yonder?" he asked with a nod of his head past the gate.

"Hmph," grunted the Indian, "Akkeekaahuush is there. She have new man in lodge. He is called Knife. Iché Shipíte want to see you."

"Wal, me'n muh partner here, we need to get ta goin', mebbe I'll stop next time," explained Knuckles as he started side stepping toward his mule.

The Indian, Holds the Enemy, stepped forward and lowered the tip of his lance just a little and said, "You come now!"

Knuckles looked to Tate, back to the Indian, and said, "Alright, alright, we'll come now." He stepped aboard his mule, leaned toward Tate and whispered, "You just stick close by and agree with ever'thin' I say. If'n ya' do, mebbe I can get us outta this mess."

"What's he want to see you about?" asked an anxious Tate, glancing back to the Indian, two others now by his side.

"Long story, but has to do with a woman," grumbled the mountain man.

Tate grinned as at the man and replied, "Couldn't be too bad, at your advanced age!"

Knuckles snapped his head around to Tate and snarled, "There ya go 'gin, bad mouthin' your betters! I ain't as old as you think, younker!"

Holds the Enemy and his two companions dog-trotted to the village to tell of the white men coming and as Knuckles and Tate rode into the central clearing, several others were gathered to see the visitors. Standing before the largest lodge were several men and a few women, all looking with somber expressions at the two white men riding into their camp. Knuckles reined up, lifted his hand beside his shoulder, palm forward and focusing his attention on the taller man in the middle, said, "greetings Iché Shipíte, I see you are now Ashbacheeítche of the River Crow. This is good!"

The chief, arrayed in buckskin leggings, a tunic with the shoulders and sleeves decorated with beads and quills, a bone and bead chest plate, a long hair decorated with tufts of fur, the front of his hair was made up with white paint making it stand a handbreadth above his forehead. He was an impressive figure as he nodded his head and said, "You are welcome Big Fist. You will stay with us?"

Knuckles knew to refuse the invitation would be an insult and he also knew he was not in a position to be anything but condescending. He nodded his head, and said, "We will be honored to stay a while," and turning to Tate he said, "This is my partner, Longbow." Tate nodded his head and waited for Knuckles to give direction. Tate had noticed the expression of a woman standing near the chief was not very friendly as she stared at Knuckles and he wondered if this was the one alluded to by his partner. As he watched, the woman turned to the chief and spoke in their language while gesturing toward the white men with obvious disagreement with the chief's invitation. The chief stared her down without speaking, causing her to spin on her heels and start away, after grabbing the vest of the man that stood near her. He followed without looking back at the white men. The chief spoke to a nearby boy, pointed away from the circle, and the boy motioned to Knuckles to follow.

The men were directed to a tipi, apparently one kept for guests, with an older woman nearby cooking some meat on a spit over her cook-fire. She waved at Knuckles, grinned and laughed, and turned back to her cooking as the men entered the tipi. They soon had their gear unloaded and stacked and bedrolls in place. Tate moved the entry flap aside and stepped out, almost bumping into the old woman. She stood before him with two wooden platters loaded with meat and vegetables, obviously for the visitors. Knuckles bumped into the back of Tate, almost knocking him into the woman, who grinned and cackled at the clumsy white men. Knuckles saw the offering, spoke to the woman in her language, thanking her for the food, and the men accepted the platters and took a seat on the ground beside the tipi.

"Wal, this shore looks better'n that cornpone stuff you're allus' a fixin'," proclaimed Knuckles.

"Go ahead, keep it up, an' you'll find yourself doin' the cookin' from here on out!" responded Tate as he filled his mouth with several prairie turnips and other greens. Knuckles already had his chompers working on his platter of food, uninterested in conversation.

When the eating slowed, and the old woman brought additional helpings, Tate sat back and said, "So, how 'bout tellin' me all about this woman trouble and what kind of a fix does it have us in?"

With juices trailing through his whiskers, Knuckles looked at his partner and began, "Wal, it were goin' on five year ago now, when I fust met up with this bunch o' River Crow. I had been trappin' in the mountains an' was makin' my way up to Fort Union, that was 'fore this hyar fort was built, to sell muh peltries. I run onto their camp an' they made me welcome right off. So, I spent a while wit' 'em, an' met up wit' a woman known as Akkeekaahuush, or Comes Toward the Near Bank, an' she was a purty'n, yessir. But, she was a war leader, and known as a mighty warrior among her people and as such, a lot o' the menfolk kinda shied away from her. But, I din't know nuthin' 'bout that kinda thing and we made eyes at each other'n hit it off. So, amongst the Crow people, the women 'er the ones what owns the lodge and she asked me to share the lodge with her. Wal, I weren't about to pass that up, so, I moved into her lodge. But what I din't know, was whenever a man does that, it's just like bein' married! When I found that out, I snuck out da' lodge late at night, got muh peltries, and skedaddled! Problem is, that Iché Shipíte, the chief, that's her brother!"

Tate chuckled a little at the tale of the old-timer and said, "So, she was the one that argued with the chief?"

"Yup, she's the one."

"Did you see when she left that she was draggin' that other feller with her?"

Knuckles looked at his friend and said, "You don't say? Wal, then, she's got her another husband! Glory be! That's why I didn't get scalped right off." He shook his head and grinned and added, "We just might get outta here O.K., then."

It was mid-afternoon when the young boy that directed them to their lodge, scratched at the entry to be admitted. When he stepped inside, he spoke to Knuckles in the Crow language, giving the chief's invitation to his lodge. Knuckles nodded his head in understanding, shared the news with Tate, and the two men stepped outside to follow the boy to the chief's lodge.

The chief, his sister, and her man called Holds the Enemy, who had a buffalo horned headdress, and three other warriors were seated on blankets, some with willow backrests, in random order outside the lodge. The chief greeted them, motioned for them to be seated, and began speaking to Knuckles in the Crow language. Tate had not noticed a young woman that seated herself slightly behind him until she began speaking softly, translating what the chief was saying. He looked back to see a very pretty, young woman in a buckskin dress with elaborate beadwork across the shoulders and down the short-fringed sleeves. She spoke excellent English and just loud enough for Tate to clearly hear her words.

The men, as the young woman translated, were just renewing old acquaintances and sharing recent experiences, much like any long-separated friends would. Then the chief raised his head to look at Tate and asked Knuckles, "Your friend is called Longbow?"

"That's right, Longbow," replied Knuckles.

"Who gave him this name?" asked the chief.

When Tate heard the question translated, he spoke up and answered, "Dohäsan, chief of the Kiowa, gave me that name."

The chief's expression showed his surprise to hear the reference to the Kiowa. His brow furrowed as he looked at Tate, wondering about this man that did not appear very old, but to have been with the Kiowa and to have been given a name of honor, was surprising. He asked, "Why did he give you that name?"

"Because I use a longbow for hunting, and he had never seen such a bow," answered Tate.

"Do you have that bow with you?" asked the chief.

"Yes, I will gladly show it to you." He stood to return to the tipi and retrieve his bow and quiver of arrows. When he approached the circle, the chief stood, as did several of the others, to examine this bow. When Tate placed the tip on his foot, the bow stood a few inches taller than the top of his head. The Indians' eyes widened as they looked, and the chief said, "Will you show us how you use it?"

"Sure," he responded and looked around for something to use as a target. The chief realized what he was doing and spoke to one of the men, who quickly left to fetch one. Tate noticed one of the men had his bow and quiver beside him and asked the chief, "Would your warrior demonstrate his bow on the target first?" The chief looked at the man, known as Uuwatchilapish, or Iron Bull, and motioned for him to place the target and take his shot. When Iron Bull returned, he grinned at the white man and said, "One arrow!" as he motioned to the target. A woven basket, turned on edge and with the bowl facing the shooter, was about three hand-breadths across and leaned against a log about forty yards distant. The man looked at Tate as he drew the arrow back on the bow, looked quickly at the target and let the arrow fly. It flew true to its mark and hit close to the center of the bowl of the basket, piercing it through and pinning it to the log.

The warrior looked at Tate smugly, and motioned for him to shoot. Tate spoke to the boy nearby, told him through the translator to take the bowl farther out until Tate motioned for him to stop. The boy looked at the translator, who nodded and motioned for him to go, and the boy trotted off to retrieve the bowl. When he picked it up, he looked back at the group and started backing up, keeping his eyes on the men and waiting for a signal. When he was almost twice the distance and the bowl was barely visible, Tate nodded, and he stopped. The boy looked around, found a few sticks to prop the basket up, arranged it for the shooter and trotted well off to the side, to stand behind a clump of sage.

Tate sat the tip of the bow on the ground beside his foot, stepped through the bow bending the upper limb down to fit the string into the nock. When strung, the bow was still almost as tall as Tate. While he was doing this, the gathered group was talking in hushed tones, pointing at the white man's long bow, with some obviously making snide remarks. He nocked an arrow, stepped forward and keeping his right hand and thumb near his cheek, he leaned his whole weight into the bow, slowly bringing it down to align the arrow with the target. As he went through his motions of drawing the bow, some of the men openly laughed at his movements, and nodded their head at the thought this man could hit the target so far away. Holding slightly over the target, he let slip the arrow that quickly whispered on its way, and buried itself squarely in the middle of the woven basket bowl. A collective gasp rose from the now frozen crowd, until they realized what he had done, and they suddenly began chattering and exclaiming, all the while gesturing to the target amazed by what they had seen. The boy ran from the sage and retrieved the arrow and basket together and ran back to give it to his chief.

When the chief looked at the basket and the still impaled arrow, he lifted his eyes to the young man and said, "It is a good name."

Knuckles, having never seen Tate use his bow, stood astounded by what he had seen the young man do, and asked, "You say you dropped a buffler wit' that?"

Tate nodded affirmative and started to unstring the bow but was stopped by the other archer who stepped beside him and asked, "I shoot bow?" Tate looked at the man who showed no animosity and said, "It is different, but yes, you can." He handed an arrow together with the bow to Iron Bull and motioned for the boy to take the target back to the first location. Iron Bull saw the boy stop and motioned him on but stopped him short of the far location. The boy placed the bowl and trotted off to the side.

Iron Bull nocked the arrow and lifted the bow to start his draw and was surprised at the tautness of the string and the difficulty in drawing it back. Tate watched and waited as the warrior gave it his all and managed to pull the string back but less than half a draw. He let the arrow fly and it wobbled wide of its mark, but farther than his shot at the first target. He looked to Tate with surprise and began jabbering and motioning to the bow, apparently remarking about how difficult it was to draw. He handed the bow back to Tate and watched as he stepped through the bow, pulled down on the upper limb to release the string and brought the bow upright. He spoke to the translator and said, "It takes many years of practice and training to use this kind of bow. The warriors of old and far away across the big waters use these bows but only for war." Iron Bull nodded his head in understanding, looking to Tate with new respect.

Knuckles said, "Wal, ya shore impressed me, younker."

The group around the chief began to disperse and Knuckles spoke to the chief to tell him they would be leaving before first light. The chief requested their presence at the evening meal and Knuckles agreed, somewhat concerned, knowing the chief's sister would probably be there as well. And he was right, but the gathering proved to be a pleasant one with Comes Toward and her husband both focused on the recent display by Tate. At her questioning, Tate began a rather lengthy explanation, made longer still by the need for translation, of the history of the longbow and its use by the archers in old England. They were somewhat skeptical of his description of the arrows sometimes piercing the armor of the enemy, but neither did they understand the use of armor. Comes Toward appeared to be satisfied with Tate's explanations and Knuckles was relieved to be free of her anticipated accusations and condemnations and was pleased she had found herself a worthy mate.

When the meal was concluded, the men stood to make their goodbyes and Tate was surprised to be given a gift by Iché Shipíte, or Black Foot, the chief of the River Crow. But it was a common practice for a respected warrior to be given honors and gifts and he was presented with a magnificent quiver made from buffalo hide. Cut from two colors of leather, fringed and beaded with both beads and porcupine quills with designs of blue outlined with white, it was an impressive piece of Crow craftsmanship. Tate was surprised, but not unprepared. After accepting the gift, he excused himself to go to the tipi and returned with a matched pair of bone handled knives, one with a unique curved blade for skinning, and the other with a long blade similar to a Bowie. Both were well crafted, and the chief was extremely pleased as he accepted the gifts. He looked at Knuckles and Tate,"You both are friends of the River Crow and will always be welcome in our villages."

As the two men mounted up and started from the village, twilight had settled across the flats and they turned in their saddles to look back at the chief and the others that were watching them leave. Knuckles looked at his partner and said, "Well younker, I'm beginnin' ta see how ya' made friends with so many o' them Injuns down South. Yessirreee."

CHAPTER FIVE
MUSTANGS

THE *PEENT, PEENT* CALL OF THE NIGHTHAWK ACCOMPANIED THE beginning of their journey into the darkness. With the moon, now beginning to wane from full, slowly rising above the rolling hills to the East, the first stars of the night shone their beckoning beacons to Tate and Knuckles as they listened to the nighthawks and the shuffling gait of the horses and mule. Letting the grulla have his head, Tate's hips rocked back and forth with his weight bringing slight creaks from the saddle leather. He was in his element, this nocturnal travel was a comfort to the young man, his eyes now accustomed to the darkness, roved the surrounding terrain, watching the shadows of darkness mark the contours of the rolling plains. A pair of antelope were silhouetted on a rise south of the travelers, watching the intruders to their territory. In the distance a pair of coyote yip yipped their calls to one another and the cicadas rattled their protests.

Tate felt at home in the darkness; the sounds, the smells, the creatures of the night, were all different than in the light. The predators were emboldened by the blanket of obscurity, and the prey, driven by their own hunger, brazenly taunted the hunters as they fed themselves and gathered more for their families. The grulla tensed as he jerked his head up, ears forward, to watch a long-legged flop-eared jackrabbit. The rabbit ran his obstacle course among the sage to escape the pursuing grey fox, the only sound the muffled thump of the rabbit's big feet beating his escape. The grulla resumed his pace, head down and ears twitching back and forth. Tate chuckled silently and reached down to pat the gelding's neck and whisper reassurances.

Their midnight break gave Tate a chance to break out some pemmican he took in trade traded from the old woman at their tipi. The men chewed on the delicacy of the desert as the horses snatched mouthfuls of grass and long drinks of water. When back on their way again, Tate's observed the trail on the south side of the river was closer to the juniper dotted hills with the many carved out ravines and gullies made rugged by the spring flash floods. They dropped from a slight knoll into a wide dry swale spotted with the short moonlit shadows outlining clusters of sage. The grulla swung his head to the side, ears pointed, and Tate looked into the blue moonlight and listened. A thunder of hooves came from the low hills and he reached for his Hawken. A quick glance told of Knuckles grabbing his as well. The men quickly slid from the saddles, keeping their mounts between them and the coming calamity, and within an instant the flaring shadows of a herd of mustangs materialized from the black. The screaming animals, nostrils flared, eyes showing white, manes flying like feathered war bonnets, charged headlong toward the men and their horses. The grulla was startled and side-stepped, reared up and knocked Tate back on his heels dropping him in the dust. The pack-horses pulled frantically at their lead ropes, rearing and kicking to get away from the melee, but the big mule stood her ground and Knuckles lay his

Hawken across the seat of the saddle and searched for a target.

The mustangs had stampeded toward the river, seeking a way of escape and the cause of that panic made itself known when a grey coated wolf launched itself at the haunches of one of the trailing horses. All the animals were in a panic, the men and their mounts had blocked the way to the river and with the pack-horses and the grulla mixing with the mustangs, hooves were flying everywhere, and the dust cloud covered everything. Several of the mustangs reared up and pawed at the darkness, squealing in protest at the night attackers, kicking back when the teeth of a wolf bit at their hocks. The pack-horses were running and bucking, trying to get away from the brawl, and Tate got to his knees, searching for a target in the dusty darkness. Suddenly a snarling maw came flying at his face and he swung the barrel of the Hawken as a club to fend off the attacking wolf. But the animal quickly found its feet and spun to attack the man again. Tate, having already set the back trigger, fired from the hip as the wolf started to jump for his throat. The canine crumpled in the air, blown back by the blast, but fell at Tate's feet.

Frantically, Tate began reloading, watchful of the battle among mustangs and wolves. He had no idea how many wolves were attacking, but he knew they would pursue their prey in a relay, and the rest of the pack might be yet to come. He heard the roar of Knuckles's Hawken and knew the old-timer had scored when he heard the whining bark of a wolf. Tate had just removed his ramrod or wiping stick, when he was bowled over by the shoulder of a terrified mustang. He rolled, keeping his grip on the Hawken, rose to his knees, once again searching for a target. He choked on the dust, wiped muddy tears from his eyes, and saw a wolf with his teeth sunk in the neck of a struggling colt. He raised the

Hawken, setting the trigger as he did, and lowered the muzzle in line with the wolf, now using his weight to try to bring the stubborn colt down. He fired and took the wolf in the neck, causing it to lose its grip on the colt, and drop to the ground.

When the mustang knocked him down, he lost his wiping stick, but reloaded, dropping a ball down the muzzle without a patch, thumped the butt on the ground to seat the ball, and searched for another target. The dust was thick, the noise deafening, horses screaming, wolves snarling and snapping, hooves clattering, and the sound of the attacking wolf was unheard by Tate. The sight of bared teeth sinking into his arm startled him and the 150 pounds of attacking wolf knocked him to the ground, with the wolf refusing to release his arm. Tate lost his grip on the Hawken, reached across his belly for the Colt, but the holster was empty! Wolf and man stared at each other, eyeball to eyeball, and Tate smelled blood, his own, saw the curled lip and snout of the angry wolf as it snarled and tried to shake his head side to side to tear at Tate's flesh. The young man reached to his back and grabbed his Bowie, brought it around and sunk it to its hilt into the chest of the massive monster. He pulled it back, drove it in again and again, but the wolf refused to let go. Tate brought the big razor-sharp Bowie up and laid it parallel to his forearm, now pulsing blood, and drew the blade across the deep fur at the muscled throat of the wolf. He knew the blade bit deep, and he felt the wolf's grip lessen. He kicked at the carcass of the beast, looked for the Hawken but had to feel for it in the thick cloud of dust.

There seemed to be no let-up to the fight. Knuckle's Hawken roared again, and mustangs screamed in protest. When Tate found his Hawken, he checked the muzzle, felt the triggers, and looked for another target. But there was none to be found. The noise lessened, and there was no snarling and snapping of wolves. Tate hoped there were no more, and the mustangs milled about, hoping the same. Tate staggered to his feet, called out for Knuckles, heard an answer, and made his way to his partner.

His mule still standing, Knuckles leaned against the faithful animal and watched as Tate materialized out of the dust cloud.

"You alright?" asked Tate, stumbling toward the man.

"Yeah, you?" responded Knuckles, wiping dust from around his eyes. Before Tate could respond, he fell forward into the dust at Knuckles feet.

THE THIN SHAFT of sunlight crowded its way through the fluttering leaves of the cottonwoods to pry open the eyes of Tate as he lay on the bedroll in the shade of the towering trees. He started to bring his hand to his face, winced at the pain of his left arm and let a low moan escape to tell Knuckles he was rousing.

"Wal, 'bout time you come 'round, younker. I was beginnin' ta think I'd hafta git some water an' splash your face to wake you up! So, how's that arm a'feelin'?"

Tate struggled to sit up, wiped his face with his right hand and looked at his bandaged elbow, squinted at his friend and said, "You tell me, you wrapped it!"

Knuckles was rolling a wolf pelt, stopped, and looked at Tate with a somber expression, "That wolf did his best to tear you apart, but lucky 'nuff, you ain't got nuthin' but gristle there, so, I think you'll heal up O.K., might take a while."

"How long's a while?" asked Tate, pulling his left elbow to his lap with his right hand.

"Wal, I made a poultice of bee balm an' milkweed, an' if'n we keep 'er clean and bandaged, mebbe a week or two."

Tate looked around the camp, noticed the horses and

mule tethered near the water. The packs and panniers were stacked under the trees, and Knuckles was busy with the wolf pelts. "How long was I out? Looks like you been purty busy."

"Wal, I still had Molly, so it weren't too hard to round up them cayuses. An, there was four of them wolves what took after them mustangs. We got 'em all, but they kilt a colt. One o' them wolves was nursin', her bags was drippin', so thar's a hungry litter o' pups out yonder some'eres." He nodded toward the rise that hid the wide draw that hid the approach of the mustangs. "These pelts'll be good tradin', Injuns really like 'em an'll give just 'bout anythin' fer 'em." He talked while he rolled up the last pelt, tied it tightly and added it to the stack of others.

Tate looked at the sun, judged it to be mid-morning, and struggled to stand. The pain in his elbow stabbed at him and he winced as he grabbed at his arm. Knuckles said, "Ya' better let me fix you up a sling so ya don't go movin' that elbow too much!"

Tate looked at his friend, nodded acceptance of his suggestion and sat back down on the log to await the old-timer's ministrations. As he looked around the campsite, he thought it would be good to take a day or two to rest up, give the stock time to recuperate, and maybe do a little exploring. He could see distant mountains on the far horizon and knew it would be another couple of days travel before they would reach the tall timber, but there was no hurry.

THE FIRST DAY was spent checking and repairing their gear, ensuring all the leather was freshly oiled and showed no weak or worn spots. They cleaned all their weapons, including the extra two Hawkens that were packed away.

After giving the animals a good rub-down with some dry grasses, the men relaxed and had an extra snooze.

The second day, Tate decided to do a little investigating, leaving Knuckles to watch the camp even though the old man's eyes were closed in slumber. Tate rode his grulla up the wide draw, backtracking the mustangs and wolves. His tracking skill was honed at an early age during the times spent in the woods with his Osage friend, Red Calf. They would often hide from one another, doing everything to cover any sign so the other would have to work out the trail with minimal left behind. His ability to track even the most difficult prey had served him well and now he watched carefully, trying to reconstruct the attack on the mustangs.

He knew that wolves are canny in that they do not follow their prey for a long distance, but plan their attack to be sudden and overwhelming, making any chase as short as possible. They are fast, but also tenacious and that attack must happen within a short distance because their stamina is not their strongest feature, but that sudden attack will usually enable them to bring down their prey within seconds.

Tate leaned from his saddle, looking at the tracks of the mustangs, saw where their first alarm caused them to suddenly dig their hooves deeper as they broke into a panicked run. The big tracks of the pursuing wolves were easily seen. Here there was sign of all four wolves, apparently the pack had attacked together, instead of the relay attack sometimes used. Tate dropped from the saddle and walked along the sandy bottom of the draw, reading the sign of the attack, the churned-up soil from the mustangs' hooves made the tracks of the wolves easy to read. Backtracking the wolves, he saw where they had lain in wait, then followed the sign to a rocky knoll, punctuated with a cluster of juniper. He stood below the knoll, surveying the massive boulders at the top. The grulla was showing a little nervousness, ears forward, eyes wide, and a bit of a twitch in his chest muscles. Tate looked at the horse, rubbed his forehead and neck, speaking softly to reassure him, and looked around for a place to tie him off. Seeing a sizable cluster of sage, he led the animal to the brush, looped the reins around a large branch, rubbed his neck again, and started toward the knoll.

He walked slowly around the rock formations, dodging the branches of the juniper as he looked for what he was certain would be there. On the back side, between two mossy boulders, was a narrow shaded cleft and he stopped back away from the hole. He waited, listened, and knew he found what he was looking for, the den of the wolves. He walked slowly and quietly to the cleft, bent around the opening and saw sign of the comings and goings of the mother wolf. He detected the smells of the wolves and bellied down to look inside. Too dark to see far, he stretched his good arm as far as he could, resting his weight on his side and hugging his injured elbow close, and suddenly jerked his arm back with an, "Why you little devil!" and reached back in the den. He grasped the furry little bundle and scooted back away from the cleft, holding a grey fur ball at arm's length. He turned around, sat the pup on his lap, holding tight to the scruff of its neck and said, "Wal, I thought there'd be more than just one, but you'll do. You're gonna come with me, maybe I'll get you somethin' to eat and see if you're worth keepin'!"

The pup was grey with black at his snout, tips of his ears, and on his feet. The long thick fur made him look bigger than he was, but his big paws supported a body that was about a foot long, plus the tail He weighed about 6 or 7 pounds. His mouth full of teeth, all of them very sharp, were displayed as he snarled and yipped at his captor. Tate tucked him back into his sling in the crook of his arm, kept him secure with his free hand, and started back to the grulla. But the horse caught the wolf smell and he started prancing nervously, but the reassuring voice of Tate settled him down as they approached. He let Shady smell the pup, which he did nervously, but finally accepted this little fur ball was no threat, and let Tate mount up without difficulty.

"So, Lobo, now we'll have to see what that old man Knuckles'll say 'boutchu."

CHAPTER SIX
COLTER'S HELL

For the past two weeks, their route lay west and south, along trails that had only been traveled by trappers and Indians. The green snake of the Yellowstone wound its way through the wide valley, with its green scales of cottonwood, larch, willows, and alder. Around them clusters of juniper, pinyon and cedar dotted the grassy plains like drops from an artist's palette that decorated the wide flats of coarse grass, prickly pear, and sagebrush. According to Knuckles, this was dangerous country, sort of an apex of territories of Gros Ventre, Nez Perce, Blackfoot, Crow and Shoshone. Tate and Knuckles knew that the many humps of boulders and juniper, or the occasional arroyo, could be the cover for an ambush. Their nocturnal travel had been a protective blanket, reassuring in its cover.

The grulla, with his muscular Morgan breeding, had quickly become accustomed to the country and took to the liberty of having his own head, as Tate let him mosey at his own pace. The previous two weeks had become monotonous and the terrain repetitious, but the distant mountain range slowly marched toward them and they now were bound to the south, with mountains on both sides, still following the Yellowstone. Tate noted the absence of any trees on the nearby flats and close in hill-sides, yet jagged shadows that marked the watershed ravines carved into the hillsides stood out like black accusing fingers pointing to the intruders to this new country.

Knuckles was leading the procession of four animals and reined up his mule to await Tate to rein alongside. As Tate moved beside him, he motioned to the front and said, "This hyar's a little easier way, we got 'bout a mile or so an' if'n I recomember right, thar's a little lake that'd be right nice campsite. We'll leave the Yellerstone, but might catch up to it a little further on."

Tate rubbed the scruffy neck of the pup, sitting across his seat behind the pommel, and said, "I'm thinkin' wher'ever we stop, we could use a little longer rest. We been in the saddle so long, muh britches are 'bout wore through!"

The old-timer chuckled at his young friend and dug heels in the ribs of his mule to once again lead off. True to his word, it was just a short while and he reined away from the smaller white-water river, following a feeder stream that splashed its way down the steeper hillside, winding through the random pines to make its way to the river below. The creek-side trail brought them to a small hanging meadow that held a crystal-clear lake with grassy shores. Knuckles turned to see the response of Tate and was pleased to see the younger man stand in his stirrups and grin ear-to-ear. The grey light of early morning was just beginning to paint the eastern sky as the men made a comfortable camp on the uphill side of the lake, under cover of a group of ponderosa and fir. They loosed the animals, knowing the fresh deep grass would keep them nearby, and began the fixings for breakfast.

"So, what was it you called this place?" asked Tate as he readied the coffee pot.

"Colter's Hell. A feller by the name of John Colter, he was with the Lewis 'n Clark bunch, after he left them he joined up wit' some other trappers whut got hit by some Blackfoot an' scattered, he come through here and lived to tell 'bout it. He saw some things that plum' skeered the buhjeebers outta him, thot he'd died n' gone to Hell. Thar's places whar the mud's boilin', water spewin', tur'ble smells, 'n such, when he told other's 'bout it, he called it fire an' brimstone, and they thot he was lyin'." Knuckles scratched at his beard, picked a biting bug from the tangled mess and popped it between his fingernails, "I thot he was lyin' too, till I come through 'n seen it fer my own self."

"I ain't seen nothin' like you're talkin' about yet," proclaimed Tate, looking askance at his friend.

"Oh, you will, younker, you shorely will. Why, there's trees that have turned to rocks, and water so hot it'd peel your skin right off, and lot's o' other things that'll make yore eyes pop right outta yo' head," declared the old man, finishing his descriptions with a cackle that made Tate remember some of the stories about witches and other goblins read to him by his father.

He looked at Lobo, who had more than doubled in size in the last two weeks, and watched as he explored and examined every nook and cranny of their campsite. He would still frolic and jump like the pup he was, but he was learning as fast as he was growing, and he never wandered far from Tate's side. He looked to the man as his parent, provider and friend, and was always watchful and attentive to his every move. Tate had begun using hand signals to start the training of the young wolf, talked to him like he understood, and rewarded him at every response.

Knuckles watched the two and understood the friendship

that was growing between man and beast was an unusual one. His original idea about the impossibility of training a wolf, well, Tate was beginning to prove him wrong. When Tate first brought the pup into camp, Knuckles was anything but pleased and argued "Nits make lice! That thing'll grow so big, he'll get hungry 'nuff, and eat your liver!" Tate had laughed him off and determined to show Knuckles how even the wildest of animals could be befriended and trained.

THE LAZY MORNING breeze came from the south and carried the stifling smell like a messenger of doom. It wasn't the smell of death, but of rotten eggs or wet matted hair, enough of a smell to bring a coughing fit as a man sucked for fresh breathable air. That wasn't supposed to happen in the clear mountain air that carried the soft scents of pine and fresh spring blossoms. Tate was instantly awake, covering his mouth and nose as he tossed off the bedroll and waved his arms and hands as if he could swim through the odor. Knuckles was sitting up, cackling at the antics of his young friend, and said, "He he he, stinks don't it? Don't worry yore head none, the breeze'll carry it away. That's them hot springs down yonder, big 'uns they is too! Come on, let's get a move on, got lotsa country ta' see!"

"I thought we were gonna rest up for a couple days?" queried Tate, looking at the old-timer rolling his bedding.

"Ah, we'll take it easy, but I don't think ya' wanna lay round here, smellin' like it is, do ye?"

Tate shook his head and began packing up their gear and the pair was on their way within moments. They continued up the river bottom, following the cascading water until they came in sight of the strangest hillside Tate had ever seen. He was reminded of a stack of irregular shaped pancakes of all different colors. Steam rose from the top of the stacked mound that showed layer after layer of colored flat-topped pools, most white but several other colors as well. Oranges, greys, yellows, pinks and greens seemed to flow like puddles of different colors. At the near edge, several elk appeared to be bedded down in shallow pools of the hot water spring. Along the edge of the mound were snags of dead trees, while others, mostly juniper, still held to their short stubby pine needles. Parts of the travertine mounds seemed to be large irregular steps that one could walk up to the top, but other areas were narrow ledges with hot water cascading down. Tate sat on the grulla, surveying the entire mound, amazed at the size of the hot water springs that formed such a sight. He looked at Knuckles, who sat grinning \, and Tate asked, "Are there others like this?"

"Not 'zactly, fer as I know, but there's other'ns whut's just as amazin' to see."

"An' those elk, don't seem to be afraid of anything!" exclaimed Tate, motioning to the royalty of the forest. There were several cows, a couple of spike bulls, and one bigger bull sporting his velvet antlers that showed promise of being a wide spread.

"Wal, they ain't seen too many people, most injuns stay shy o' this place, think it's inhabited by strange spirits. I did too, first time I came thru hyar wit' Joe Meek. We was camped a bit further south, an' in the middle o' the night, the ground started in ta' shakin' and roarin', I thought the devil his self was comin' after me, shore 'nuff!"

"What happened?"

"It was the devil! He got me by the beard, looked at me, spit on the ground and said he didn't want me, cuz I was too blamed ornery! He he he. Next mornin' we went ta' lookin' round an' found whut they calls a geyser! That's whar, ever so often, the hot water shoots way up in th' air and makes a terrible noise and shakes the ground an' ever'thin'."

"Jumpin' jehosaphat, old man, you keep blowin' off that hot air, you're gonna make those hot springs dry up in embarrassment. So, what say we move along an' you can find somethin' else to tell lies about."

"Why you young whippersnapper, I'll just show you. Now, see if'n you can keep up with this old man!" He gigged his mule and trotted into the trees, with a backward glance to see if Tate was following. His young partner gave the grulla his head and followed after the mule riding mountain man, tugging his pack horse behind. Though Knuckles wouldn't admit it, this place gave him a strong case of the willies, not that he believed in spirits of the area like the Indians, but the different anomalies made him fearful. Like most men of the mountains, he wanted to be in control and wasn't comfortable with the unknown. He kept up a quick pace through the timber, and when the trees cleared, he kicked the mule into an easy lope. By late morning, the horses were breaking into a lather and Tate called for a stop. The only break taken by Knuckles was mid-morning when they came near what he called mud-pots; big pools of thick grey/blue mud that boiled with big air bubbles splattering to the edges of the pools. Tate had remarked, "I see why Colter described this as fire and brimstone. I ain't never seen the like."

When Knuckles reined up at the edge of a clearing on the shoulder of the hill, he dropped to the ground and undid the saddles and packs, slipping them from the horses and making a stack by the trees. Tate followed suit and all the animals rolled in the grass, rose and started their graze. Tate grabbed a handful of dry grass and began rubbing down his grulla and while the horse enjoyed the attention, he didn't stop eating. After tending to both the pack horses, he started for Molly but was stopped by Knuckles with, "Don't go spoilin' her! You do that an' she'll be 'spectin' it all the time."

Tate grinned at his friend, dropped the handful of dry

grass, and sat down in the shade with Knuckles. "This sure is an amazing country, but I'm thinkin' I agree with you, wouldn't be anywhere I'd wanna stay for long."

"Nope, stinks too much fer me. I like the clean mountain air whut ain't stunk up wit' these fountain thingamajigs."

Tate walked to the edge of the clearing, looked at the valley below, spotted several steam plumes that marked the hot water springs and mud pots and scanned the opposite hillside and surrounding area. He turned back to Knuckles and said, "How 'bout we spend the night here, give the horses a rest, and make an easy day tomorrow?"

"Sounds fine to me. Onliest thang I wanted you ta' see was the big spout, an' it ain't too fer away, might even feel the darned thing from hyar."

"Well, this is a good spot, I can see a couple game trails below us, we got fresh water over yonder," motioning with a head-nod to the little creek that tumbled down the slope beside them, "and there's plenty of grass. We can have our meal 'fore it gets dark and let the trees filter out the smoke, so it won't be seen, not that there's anybody to see it, so we should be alright."

They brought the horses closer to camp as the twilight faded, strung a picket line between two big spruce, and stretched out on their bedrolls nearby. It took awhile for Tate to drop off, Knuckles made enough noise with his snoring he thought it would scare any night critters away, but it wasn't the noise as much as that recurring feeling that something was pulling him on, some nagging sensation that there was something or someone waiting for him and he couldn't sort it out. It was shy of midnight when Tate finally dropped off and the only sound was the occasional snore of the old-timer that was out-of-tune with the clear cry of the nighthawk.

In the dark of the night, Tate stirred awake, moving only his eyes, he heard the low growl of Lobo, lying next to him with head up, and looking toward the picket line. Lying on his side, Tate listened and watched the horses. With ears forward, nostrils flared, and nervously side-stepping, they showed fear. Tate knew this was not the fear of man, but an animal. Something was approaching the camp and the horses didn't like it; they tugged at their tethers, and Tate rolled from his blankets. He heard the click of Knuckles setting his triggers and Tate did the same, searching the blackness of the trees for any sign of attack. Knuckles whispered, "Grizz, I can smell him!" The old-timer rose to one knee, using the uplifted knee as a rest for his arm and the Hawken, Tate stood and stepped beside the smooth barked spruce.

Suddenly, the roar of the charging Grizzly shattered the stillness of the night. Horses screamed and jerked at the picket line. Knuckles's Hawken roared, and smoke belched from the muzzle, but almost before the lead ball left the muzzle, Knuckles had dropped the butt to the ground and was reloading. The bear roared again, and the squeal of a horse told of attack. The animal kicked back and the thump of hooves against the grizzly was heard as the big bear coughed a growl. The bear was soon draped over the rump of one of the pack horses, claws digging into flesh, teeth bared and biting, and hideous sounds coming from both horse and bear. Tate fired his Hawken at the neck of the bear, heard the bullet strike, but the monster dug his claws deeper and sunk his teeth into the torn flesh.

Knuckles rose and stepped to the side, searching for a better shot, but his line of fire was blocked by the panicked and kicking horses. His mule had jerked free and fled, but the second pack horse was stretched out, pulling at the tethered lead rope, eyes showing white and nostrils flared. He frantically dug in his hooves trying to get away from the mauling bear. Knuckles fired and scored another hit, but the stubborn silver-tip would not release its grip on the bloody gelding.

Tate was hurriedly reloading, saw the bear lift its head to look at Knuckles and appeared to be readying to charge the man. Tate had just rammed home the .54 caliber ball, brought his rifle up and just as the bear started to drop to all fours to attack Knuckles, Tate fired from the hip and the lead ball sent the ramrod flying into the thick fur of the grizz and drove it home. The bear started to stand, swatting at the offending wiping stick, growling and snarling at this new attacker, and turned to charge. Tate drew his Paterson and fired, and fired again, until the pistol was empty, and the bloody beast staggered, sliding his chin on the ground almost at Tate's feet.

Knuckles, finishing reloading his rifle, tucked the wiping stick away and walked slowly to the side of the bear, muzzle pointed at the back of its head, and poked the animal, ensuring it was dead. Lobo jumped at the bear's carcass, growling and snapping, tearing at the fur. Both men grinned and let out a long sigh as they stood up and placed the butts of their rifles beside their bare feet and looked at the monstrous beast before them.

"Whew, that's enough to make a man get religion!" declared Knuckles.

Tate chuckled and replied, "Oh, I was askin' the Lord to help us, you betcha!"

The men walked to the injured pack horse, still tethered but shaking and dripping blood. After looking the animal over with the aid of a firebrand, Knuckles said, "I'll take him out yonder and take care o' him. You can start workin' on ol' Ephraim, there," nodding to the Grizzly. Within moments, Tate heard the report of Knuckles Hawken, and the man returned, carrying the halter and lead rope. Tate had begun the work of skinning the grizzly, pushing Lobo aside but still letting the pup work at killing the already dead grizzly, and Knuckles silently joined in the task.

CHAPTER SEVEN
SHOSHONE

"NOW WE'RE IN A FIX, SURE'S SHOOTIN'!" SAID KNUCKLES AS HE stood to stretch and take a short break from skinning the massive grizzly. "What with onliest one pack horse, we ain't gonna be carryin' all whut we gots," he mumbled as he waved his hand around at their packs and gear. "An' 'sides, add this hyar hide to the lot, hummmm, dunno, just dunno." He shook his head and dropped to his knees to resume his part of the skinning of the stinking bear. In the wilderness, all bears repeatedly mark their territory with urine and by rubbing their scent glands on trees and rocks. They are also carrion eaters and they develop a distinctive smell or stench that is easily identified. That stink made the task of skinning more difficult and neither man could stand it for long, taking several breaks during the deed.

"Well, I haven't seen any sign of mustangs here 'bouts, so if you have any ideas, let's hear 'em," declared Tate.

"Ya know, as I think 'bout it, them Crow wimmen was able to travel 'round and packin' ever' thin' they owned, lodge an' all. They dun' it wit' a travois, mebbe we need ta' make us up one o' them."

Tate leaned back on his haunches, looked at the old-timer as he waved away a fly from his face, and said, "Best idea you had all day. But we'll still need to split up the packs and lighten the load a mite. We seem to be takin' on more'n we're usin'," surmised Tate. When he resupplied on his trip to St. Louis, he added a good amount of trade goods, hoping to use trading as a way of getting acquainted with the different tribes. The only trade that happened so far was with the Crow and it was more of an even-up exchange. With two pack-saddles, panniers, and parfleches, it was difficult to separate the load with some on Shady and Molly and the remainder on the pack-horse with the travois.

The travois, made with two long slender lodge-pole pines cut from above their last camp, hung from the withers of the pack horse and extended well behind. The men had added some padding to the shoulders for the horse, preventing the poles from rubbing, and made a basket weave of strips of deer hide for the platform, giving a sizeable flat for stacking the goods. With the large bear hide and the four wolf pelts taking almost half the space, they carefully packed the remainder of their gear and covered it all with an oil cloth used for a ground cover. Satisfied with their work, Knuckles looked it over and proclaimed, "Why we'uns'd make good squaws, yessiree. Ain't never seen no squaw do better'n that."

Tate shook his head at the old man and observed, "This will make it harder to take some o' them narrow trails. That means we'll be travelin' in the open more. Mebbe we need to go back to travelin' by the moonlight."

"Oh now, don't go gettin' all flustered. This hyar's Shoshone country, an' I know some o' them. Spent a winter wit' 'em oncet."

"The last time we ran into some of your old Indian friends, it didn't start out too good. Did you have another woman problem with the Shoshone?"

"He he he," cackled the old-timer as he grinned at his partner, "Weren't no problem 'cep had ta' fight 'em off. They was so many o' them fine wimmin' folks, they was just fightin' fer the chance to spend time wit' me. He, he, he."

"Are there any tribes in these mountains you didn't have troubles with?" asked Tate.

"Them ain't troubles, boy, them's shinin' times. Yessireee bob!"

MID-DAY SAW the two men taking a break for coffee and pemmican, giving the animals a time for some graze and a roll before continuing. They sat under the long limbs of a ponderosa, leaning back against the rough bark, trying to avoid the sap, and sipped the black brew to wash down the pemmican. The morning's trail stayed near a small creek that hung alongside a long bluff that led to a wide plateau to the west. Several plumes of steam told of hot springs and other geothermal sites, while chalk flats told of the spread of the death waters, as Knuckles called them. Tate had taken a big gulp of coffee, when the ground began to vibrate, startling him so that he spat out the coffee and spilled his cup. He leaned forward to avoid the coffee, looked at Knuckles, who was laughing at the antics of his young partner, and with his facial expression and lifted shoulders asked what was happening. When Knuckles quit laughing, he stuttered, "He, he, he, that's whut I was tellin' you 'bout! Lookee yonder!" he instructed as he pointed toward the white chalky flat.

Tate stood to look and saw what appeared as a cauldron of water boiling and splashing in the midst of the white mound below them. As he watched, Knuckles stood alongside. The water, looking light turquoise colored, began to dance and boil higher and higher. Suddenly, a massive spout of water shot skyward, taller than any of the trees anywhere near. Tate estimated the water to spew well over two hundred feet high. The accompanying roar echoed back from the hillsides and sounded like an approaching thunderstorm. The fountain continued to boil high and roar like a tumbling waterfall and Tate stood amazed with wonder written on his face. "Would you look at that!" he muttered, almost to himself. Both men stood mesmerized, never noticing the horses and mule also watching in wonder. As the geyser began to falter, the men relaxed and sat back down to finish their bit of grub and a fresh cup of java.

"You know, my Pa wanted to see the mountains more'n anybody I know. But if he was still alive and I told him about what I've seen in these past few days, I don't think he'd believe a word ," mused Tate.

"Wal, tha's prob'ly true. When I first heard them stories that was told by Colter, I didn't believe it, had ta' see it muh ownself. E'en tho' I seen it couple times now, still hard to believe." He looked around at the animals, tossed the dregs of his coffee at the low burning coals, and said, "Wal, c'mon younker, unless I disremember, I'ma thinkin' we might find us a Shoshone camp south a here. Might e'en make it fore dark."

"Are you sure you wanna do that? Wouldn't it be better to check it out in the daylight, make sure there's no mad women stompin' around waitin' for you to show up so they can lift your hair?"

"Awww, hogwash! They's prob'ly sittin' by the trail, lookin' yonder ways, hopin' I'd show up and let 'em love on me a while!"

"Well, if we find their camp, I'll hang back and watch, just in case they have other plans for you," jawed the younger man, grinning at the whiskered face of his counterpart.

They followed the trail alongside the narrow river that led to the top of the wide plateau. Travel was easier, especially with the travois, but it was farther than Knuckles had calculated. Midmorning of the second day, they looked down from the plateau and watched the activity of the Shoshone encampment. With over a hundred lodges, the village hummed with children playing, women working at cookfires and scraping hides, men working with horses and fashioning weaponry, and youngsters moving a sizable horse herd into a nearby valley for graze. Tate used his spyglass to survey the village, and said, "Well, I don't see any women wavin' lances or doin' a war dance. You might be safe after all," he kidded the old-timer. Even though Knuckles was considerably older than Tate, the best he could remember he was only in his early forties. The harsh winters and hard living had robbed his hair and whiskers of their color and the grey at his chin made him appear older. To answer Tate's taunt, Knuckles gigged his mule and started down the hillside, following the easy trail that led to the bottom. Tate followed close behind, leading the pack horse with the travois.

As they neared the village, two men of the dog soldier warrior society who had been on watch, rode alongside Knuckles and challenged him with lances bearing scalps. Knuckles shook his fist at them and answered in their tongue, somewhat angrily. The two warriors laughed at the man and motioned for him to follow. When they were led into the encampment, several people walked toward them, forming a pathway to the central circle of tipis. Some of the people called out a greeting to Big Fist in their language, most seemed to be friendly. When they entered the circle, Knuckles called out, "Owitze! Greetings my friend!" as he lifted his hand in greeting. Standing in front of a large tipi, was a small group of stoic warriors, attired in buckskin leggings, breechcloths, some with beaded vests and others with bone and bead breastplates. The warrior in the middle, Owitze, or Twisted Hand, was apparently the chief and at his side stood his war chief, Aingabite Bia'isa, Red Wolf. On the other side was the chief of the dog soldiers, Po'have, or The Horse. They were an impressive trio and stood unmoving at the approach of the white men. Knuckles said, "We have come to trade with the great Kuccuntikka Shoshone."

Knuckles sat waiting and the moment of silence seemed to stretch until Twisted Hand slowly lifted his hand and said, "Big Fist. It has been many summers since we have seen you. Get down, we will eat and talk. Tomorrow, we trade. My sister, Pinaquanah, will be glad to see you."

Tate dropped his head and thought, *Here it comes. Another mad woman gonna do us in!* He lifted his head to see a woman step to the side of Knuckles and place her hand on his knee as she looked up at the man. "Pinaquanah is glad to see her man," she said proudly as she looked at the whiskered face man. Knuckles looked down at her and smiled and replied, "Why, Smells of Sugar, you are a sight fer sore eyes, yessiree."

"You will come with me, and your friend too," she ordered with a head nod toward Tate. Knuckles looked to his friend and said, "Guess we better do as she says. She ain't the chief's sister, they call all their relatives that, I think she's a cousin 'er sumpin', but she's a good cook, that's fer certain."

Sugar led the men to her lodge, near the outside edge of the village, helped them unload the horses and after dropping the travois beside the lodge, she directed Tate to take the horses and mule to the horse herd to be watched over by the young men of the village. On his way back to the lodge, Tate attracted a following and several youngsters and others were surprised to see this white man with a wolf pup following. The pup was growing rapidly and had no difficulty keeping up with the long-legged man, staying right at his heels, unconcerned with the many onlookers.

When Tate returned to the lodge, he was surprised to see a small boy of about three or four, squatting on his heels by the fire, watching the woman prepare the meal. He often asked questions, never changing his stance, motioned to Knuckles and then to Tate as he spoke softly to his mother. Tate looked questioningly at Knuckles who shrugged his shoulders, and both looked back at the woman. She stood from the fire, retrieved a couple of bark platters, filled them with a stew of meat and wild vegetables and handed one to the boy, motioned for him to take it to Tate. When he returned, she handed him the second platter and said in English, "Take that to your father," and pointed to Knuckles. Tate almost dropped his platter and watched as Knuckles sat upright, looking at Sugar. She smiled at him, motioned to the boy, and Knuckles looked at the youngster, accepted the platter, leaned back against the log sitting motionless for several minutes.

Finally, he looked at Tate, who was busy with eating, then back at the woman, and asked, "So, you're sayin' he's muh son?"

She nodded her head with a coy smile and said, "He is called Chochoco, Has no Horse, until his father gives him a proper name." Knuckles looked at the boy, back to the woman, and over at Tate with a scared expression on his face. Tate said, "No trouble, huh?" and resumed his eating, trying to keep from laughing.

CHAPTER EIGHT
ALONE

"WAL, YOUNKER, WHEN WE HOOKED UP TOGETHER, I TOL' YA' I was just gonna be wit'chu till we got to the mountains. Wal, we been in the mountains a while now."

Tate chuckled and replied, "I know, I know, but you're kinda like a bad habit. One ya' know ya' need to get shuck of, but hard to do, ya' know what I mean?"

"You know I wouldn't be doin' it, but I never knowed I had a young'un o' muh own."

"You're right, Knuckles, you need to stay with your family. That boy needs a father, too bad he's gotta settle for you," Tate said with a wide grin.

Knuckles knew the younger man was kidding him, but he replied, "It's too bad we ain't gonna be together, cuz this father'd have to take down yore britches an' tan yo' hide!"

Tate turned away from his grulla, reached for the packs on the first pack horse, checked the rigging and went to the second, the new addition to his string. He had worked a trade with Po'have, the Horse, for two horses and some newly crafted iron tipped arrows. The wolf pelts and some geegaws for his squaw had pleased the man, who was known as one of the best craftsmen of arrows in the village. He was surprised when Tate asked for arrows that were more than a full handbreadth longer than the usual arrows, but he was so excited about the wolf pelts and his happy wife with the beads, vermillion, and mirror, he did as he was asked. Tate chose to leave the grizzly hide for Knuckles, knowing the stories he would tell would enhance his standing with the Shoshone, and Tate didn't want to pack the heavy hide and didn't have an inclination to spend the time tanning it anyway. Tate now had his own saddle horse, two pack horses and a spare mount, for his string.

He looked at the old-timer and stretched out a hand to shake, but Knuckles knocked it aside and the two shared a bear hug with back slaps, pushed apart and held each other at arm's length and Knuckles stepped back. "Now remember, you head straight south across that plateau an' you'll come to a river. Foller it downstream and you'll come to a big ol' lake with a row o' craggy mountains behin' it. Go along the east bank o' that lake, turn directly east, put them mountains to yer back, an' you'll be a'pointin' right at the cut in them mountains that'll take you o'er to the Wind river. That'll put'chu on the east o' them Wind River mountains."

Tate interrupted and asked, "Uh, the mountains by the lake, how'll I make 'em out ta' be sure I got the right mountains an' the right lake?"

"Wal, they been called a lot o'names, but nuttin's stuck. One ol' tale has it that's whar they buried the devil, an' he stuck his hand up to try ta' get out but didn't make it. Them mountains look just like the tips of his fingers stickin' up, like this." Knuckles held his hand up, palm forward, fingers spread and pointed at the four finger tips. "Four o' them thar' rough lookin' crags a stickin' up just like that."

Tate nodded his head in understanding and Knuckles continued, "Now, when ya' git o'er that pass, and ya see the

Wind river, if'n I was you, I'd kinda stay close to the tree-line 'longside them Wind River mountains. That big ol' flat whar the river winds, ain't got much cover, less'n you be a jackrabbit o'er a antelope."

Tate stepped to the stirrup and swung aboard the grulla, he turned to the old-timer, with Pinaquanáh at his side, and said, "We'll be seein' you, my friend."

"You betcha, an' when yore down in them Winds, you watch yore topknot, that there's Arapaho country. Sometimes they's friendly, sometimes they just want to lift yore hair. So, keep your topknot on, y'hear?"

Tate waved at his friend, reined the grulla around and led the string of horses from the camp, Lobo on his pommel, and waved again at his friend. He lifted his eyes to the trail that led up the bluff to the wide plateau and dug heels into the grulla's sides to quicken the pace. He was alone again and looked forward to the solitude, knowing the only ones to share his time in the wilderness would be Lobo, Shady, and the other horses. He smiled at the thought, breathed deep of the pine scented air, and looked at the blue sky peeking through the thick pines at the crest of the bluff.

When Knuckles had instructed him to stand with his back to the lake and the mountains, he told Tate he would be at the bank of the Snake river. "As you look upstream, that thar's the headwaters o' the Snake. That's the direction you wanna go." Late afternoon found Tate at the edge of the river and he reined the grulla to follow the river into the timber beyond. At the confluence of three forks, Tate took the center fork, as instructed by his friend, following a well-used game trail, but keeping the stream in sight.

By the time the setting sun made silhouettes of the rugged mountains behind him, Tate found a campsite at the base of a bluff, well protected in the trees but near the stream. He savored his solitude, but admitted he missed the companionship of Knuckles. He started his fire, put on the coffeepot, sat the skillet near the flames and put in some bear fat to fry up the last of the deer meat. He sliced some turnips and onions into the pan and sat back to take in his surroundings. As he looked to the valley below, he saw a couple of deer tip-toeing to the water, a wide winged hawk circling overhead and a beautiful vista of the distant mountains he left behind. And he felt again, the tugging at his spirit of something drawing him on, something that seemed like an unsatisfied hunger or yearning. He shook his head, unknowing, and wondering. All he could do was follow his heart, maybe he would discover what it was soon.

After a well-deserved night's rest, Tate sat on a log, holding a cup of steaming coffee in one hand and playing with the pup with the other. Lobo would fetch a tossed stick, return to Tate's side with high jumping bounds and drop the stick at his feet, then stretch out his front legs, lay his jowls between his big feet, rump in the air and roll his eyes at his master, waiting for another chance to fetch the stick. The pup was growing fast and already stood mid-calf to Tate, he had lost most of his puppy fur, and was developing a smooth silky coat of grey. He was taking on the look of an adult wolf, but still had the personality and behavior of a pup. Tate guessed it would be at least a couple of months before the pup was gone and a full-grown wolf took his place. But he just couldn't see his four-legged friend as a vicious wolf.

Tate picked up the stick and reached back, readying his throw, when he felt the ground begin to vibrate. His first thought was of another geyser somewhere near, but the movement increased, and he began to hear a rumble, different from a geyser. He stood, looking around and turned back to look up the bluff behind his camp, a cloud of dust was rising, and the rumble increased, he thought stampede! But what? What was stampeding? Then he heard sounds of something falling and screams and war whoops, and his confusion caused him to look around again to find the source of the commotion. Bellers, screams, and the sound of rocks sliding came from behind an outthrust of the bluff to the east of his camp and a billowing cloud of dust rose. He stepped up on the log to see above the trees between him and the bluff, and looking at the top ridge, he saw a fleeting figure of a mounted Indian. He dropped down and stepped closer to the trees to hide himself from sight. He looked around nervously, seeing to the horses as they stood at the picket line, nervously flicking ears back and forth and side stepping a little. Lobo was at his side, looking up to see what was happening, occasionally whimpering.

Reassured his animals were well tethered and out of sight of anyone from atop the bluff or from below by anyone near the river, he decided he best take a closer look at what was happening. He slipped his Hawken from its scabbard, checked the load and cap, donned his powder horn and possibles bag, slipped on his Paterson and Bowie, and stepped off into the trees with Lobo at his heels. He stealthily worked his way atop the outthrust of the bluff, utilizing a thick cluster of juniper just at the edge for cover. He bellied down as he approached the crest and slowly peeked over at the commotion.

The bluff above had a sheer drop-off of close to a hundred feet. At the top edge were several warriors, shouting and shaking their lances in jubilation at the scene below them. At the bottom of the bluff was an unbelievable mound of dead and dying buffalo. Scampering around were dozens of women and youngsters and several warriors, working their way to the pile of brown and bloody beasts to begin their butchering work. Tate looked on in wonder. He had heard of buffalo jumps but had never seen one. Here was living proof of what he had been told and never believed.

The Indians, and he didn't know what tribe they were, had used this method for decades, even centuries, to make a mass kill that would provide meat and other needs for an entire village for months to come. Before the coming of the white man and his rifles, this was the most effective way to have a sizable kill for a large village. By herding the buffalo together and stampeding them over the jump, whether it be a cliff or bluff, they would provide for the many families of the village for some time. Tate shook his head at the carnage but reminded himself it was no different than the mass kills he had both witnessed and heard about by the white man. This way, every part of the animal would be used and nothing would be wasted like when the white man took only the hide and left the carcass to rot.

He crabbed his way back from the edge, then worked his way back to his camp. He knew the buffalo hunters would be busy all day and perhaps longer and they were right in his path to the pass over the mountains. He looked down at Lobo and said, "Well boy, looks like we got us a day or two to rest up and relax. Maybe this evenin' I'll take my bow and see if I can find us some fresh meat back yonder away from all these buffalo eatin' folks." The wolf pup jumped up alongside his master acting as if he understood every word, and who knew? Maybe he did.

CHAPTER NINE
WAGONS

ELEVEN WHITE TOPPED WAGONS WOUND LIKE A LAZY SNAKE AS it followed the North Platte River away from Fort William. The fort had been the last supply stop on their journey to Oregon territory. With well over a month on the trail already, all were anxious to make it to and across the Rocky Mountains. On a clear day, they could see the distant jagged horizon that marked the far mountains, and the sight encouraged them after so many days of tiresome travel. The lead wagons, seven of them, each pulled by six mules, were supply wagons belonging to Milton Sublette and Thomas Fitzpatrick, bound for the Rendezvous with fur trappers in the Wind River mountains. Separating the supply wagons from the others was a two-wheeled cart that carried the lame Sublette, having lost a leg and now walking on a cork leg made by a friend. The last four wagons, each pulled by four mules, belonged to missionaries from the American Board of Commissioners for Foreign Missions and bound for the Nez Perce Indians in the uncharted territories.

Each of the heavy supply wagons was driven by an experienced and hand-picked muleskinner and most also carried a teamster to help with the load of supplies and to serve as relief driver if needed. The missionaries handled their own wagons with Marcus Whitman and his wife, Narcissa, in the lead and followed by Henry Spalding and his wife, Eliza. The third wagon was driven by William Gray, who traveled alone, and the last wagon held the Price family, Nathan, Amy, and their daughter, Melissa.

Marcus Whitman, a physician, was the only one that was not new to this country. Just two years before he had traveled with another missionary and ministered to the Flathead and Nez Perce nations, promising to return with other missionaries and teachers to live and work with them. He was now returning with a new wife and another missionary couple, the Spaldings. William Gray and the Price family were lay people and volunteers to help with the mission work.

Aside from the muleskinners, teamsters, and missionaries, William Sublette had hired two experienced mountain men to serve as scouts and hunters. Both had been trappers and knew the area where they were bound. One was a Frenchman who called himself Jacques, and his partner was known as Thumbs, having lost one of his thumbs during a captivity with the Arapaho. Although somewhat surly, the men seemed capable enough and kept to themselves.

"I know, I know, Marcus, but I still don't like it. That man just, just, well, everything about him makes me cringe. He's dirty and coarse, and have you noticed, every time he passes by he stares at me? And just yesterday, Melissa Price told me that both of those men ogled her and made unseemly remarks!" stated Narcissa Whitman, complaining to her husband.

"What kind of 'unseemly' remarks?" inquired Marcus, wondering about the statement from the flirtatious young woman. Although he had no concerns regarding the Price couple and their commitment to this mission work, he wasn't as certain about their daughter, who was an attractive and coquettish type of a girl.

"Well, I don't know exactly, but I'm sure it was rather coarse, coming from those two!"

"I'm certain we have nothing to be concerned about. Mr. Sublette seems to be well in control of the entire wagon train and he has assured me, he will tolerate no misbehavior from any of his men. Now, we've been fine for the past five weeks, and I'm confident the rest of the journey will be just as safe. Mr. Sublette has the utmost confidence in the two scouts, and we can't expect them to behave as if they were on the streets of Boston. Those men have spent most of their adult lives in the mountains with nothing but other trappers, uncivilized Indians, and wild animals. We can't expect too much of them, now, and don't forget, as missionaries we should be concerned for the souls of everyone we meet, including those two."

Narcissa felt like she had been scolded and dropped her head, mumbling, "I'm sorry. You're right. That's the same thing they said at the mission board. I guess I still have a lot to learn."

Marcus looked at his contrite wife, reached down to pat her knee, that was padded by several layers of clothing. His wife was the model of modesty and never showed any skin except from her wrists down and her chin up, and even then, that was seldom seen as she hid her face under a bonnet and quite often wore gloves. He was pleased with his young wife and knew they would be a great couple and would work well together as they sought to fulfill the Lord's will as they ministered to the native people. He had spent a lot of time in prayer for the right partner for his life, and for the right workers for the mission. He repeatedly praised his Lord for the prompt answer to prayer.

Henry Spalding was a stern looking man with a receding hairline and full beard that gave a look of maturity beyond his years. His entire life had been devoted to the work of his Lord and he never thought of doing anything but being a preacher of the Gospel. After his formal education at Western Reserve College, he married his sweetheart and entered the Lane Theological Seminary, but his meeting with Marcus Whitman changed the direction of the Spaldings' lives when they joined the Whitmans, received an appointment with the mission board, and departed for the west. His wife, Eliza, and Narcissa Whitman had quickly become fast friends, and were almost inseparable whenever the wagons stopped. He was glad his wife would have the companionship of another woman, as they would be the only white women in the mission work. Of course, Mrs. Price and her daughter would be there, but they were lay workers and not as committed as Eliza and Narcissa.

Nathan Price had been a farmer, in partnership with his brother, Samuel. But the farm, left to Samuel, the eldest, when their father passed, although very productive, was not providing for two growing families, and Samuel and his brother were often at odds with one another over the new found religion of Nathan. When the opportunity was given for them to join the mission work, his family eagerly accepted. He had been told his experience with farming would be a godsend for the mission and the native peoples. He was told of the fertile country and ample spaces for him to establish his own farm, even larger than his home place, and it would also be used to teach the Nez Perce about cultivating crops, giving him a lot of extra needed labor. It was a dream come true, and to work alongside of missionaries was an answer to prayer.

William Gray, although traveling alone, had committed to at least two years to work with the mission. He had heard much about the Oregon territory and was anxious to see the country and be a builder of a new state. His ambition ran more to politics and business, but he was pleased to have the opportunity to work with the mission and learn about the territory. He knew he would be among the earliest settlers, and as such, would have his choice of locations for a townsite and home. He was the type of visionary the new country needed.

As they sat around the fire that night, the conversation centered on the route they were taking and the time remaining on the trip. Sublette had joined the group of missionaries, preferring the cooking of Eliza and Narcissa to that of the teamster cook for the rest of the wagons. He began his explanation, "So, that's still the North Platte that we been follerin' all 'cross Nebrasky and now in the territories. We'll keep follerin' it till it turns south, then we'll take the Sweetwater river on west and make our way to South Pass at the tail end of the Wind River mountains. We'll cross o'er the pass, an' couple days after that, we'll be at the Rendezvous. That's where we'll be splittin' up an you can go on north to the Nez Perce country."

"How long do you think that'll be?" asked Narcissa.

"Wal, it'll be just a little more'n a week 'fore we hit the Sweetwater, 'bout the same, mebbe a little less, 'fore we get to South Pass, and then 'bout four or five days to the Rendezvous. So, all told, 'bout three weeks 'fore we split up."

"Have you been through this country often?" asked Eliza.

"Yes'm, many times. First as a trapper, then with muh brother and Jedediah Smith, we put together a fur comp'ny, and you know about Fort William back yonder, we built that, but this venture called and I thot I'd make at least one more trip for a rendezvous. The price of beaver had gone down so much, ain't hardly worth the trouble."

"Those two men you have scouting for you, Jacques and Thumbs, have you known them long?" asked Narcissa.

"No m'am, but they's alright. I knowed 'bout 'em, and like lots o' trappers, since the price on peltries dropped, most trappers cain't hardly make a livin' no more so they gotta find other work, like scoutin' an' huntin' an' such. They ain't no differ'nt'n most others."

"Now, if you folk'sll 'scuse me, I need ta' check on the men 'fore we turn in for the evenin', gotta set out guards cuz we're gettin' into Injun country." He used his crutch to straighten up and walked away from the firelight.

As they watched him go, Narcissa turned to her husband and said, "Alright, maybe I was wrong. Expecting mountain men to act even a little civilized is too much."

Henry Spalding cocked an eyebrow at her remark and Marcus felt obliged to explain. After hearing about their previous conversation, Henry said, "Yes, you should be careful, but be careful about being judgmental. All of us have faults and shortcomings, but it takes the rest of us to help one another along." Narcissa turned away from Reverend Spalding and looked at her husband, grinned, and stuck out her tongue at him. He chuckled at her response and shook his finger at her as he grinned back, letting a another low chuckle escape, unheard by the others.

She thought to herself, asking, *Do I have it in me to tolerate those men for another three weeks? Humm, into each life a little rain must fall.*

CHAPTER TEN
TRAPPERS

It was the time of day Tate enjoyed most, with the sun slowly dropping from the wide expanse of clear blue sky, making its way to the ragged granite peaks that clawed at the heavens. The cloudless sky was slowly donning the colors of end-of-day, but the absence of canvas clouds to paint offered little more than the hint of coming night. Tate was belly down at the edge of the tall grass embankment that stretched toward the edge of the bluff and the sloping hillside behind it. He watched as the different animals cautiously worked their way to their evening drink from the chuckling stream.

From across the flat came a small herd of wapiti, mostly cows and new calves with a few yearling bulls, unafraid of any predator. They relied on their senses to give ample warning, knowing the open flats behind them gave them a clear route of escape. Even the grizzly had not the stamina to keep up with the fleet-footed elk. The bear was faster for short distances, but with a clear field, the elk could easily out-distance one. On the near side of the stream, Tate was surprised to see a bunch of bighorn sheep bravely marching to the water's edge. He had been waiting for something smaller than an elk, thinking he would easily find a deer, but he was pleased at the opportunity to take a bighorn. He noted the path they'd taken to the water, thinking they would surely return to the higher mountain range the same way, and as they neared the water, he stealthily made his way nearer the return path.

The sheep drank their fill and paused for a couple of mouthfuls of graze, then lazily pointed to the mountains, pushed by the big full curl ram at the back. The ewes and lambs trotted between the scrub oak, following the trail that would lead to safety. Tate was hidden behind a scraggly cedar and stepped into his bow, bringing the arrow to full draw, just as a young ram pushed against the herd to mimic the moves of the herd ram. The arrow whispered its way to impale itself into the rib cage of the young ram, it jumped and fell in a heap at the side of the trail. The move alarmed the herd and within seconds the entire bunch had disappeared into the black timber that climbed the mountainside.

Tate looked around to see if anyone or anything had witnessed the kill. Seeing nothing, he walked to the downed ram, Lobo following at his side. In a short while, he had the ram field-dressed and with the carcass over his shoulders, started back to the camp. Lobo had taken his fill of the fresh offal and now followed at the heels of his master.

Unknown to Tate, he had been seen by one of the Arapaho warriors on scout around their camp. That warrior, Little Raven, was surprised to see a white man use a bow to take a ram, and from that distance, showing considerable marksmanship, and to have a wolf pup following, this was indeed an unusual white man.

Back at camp, and hungry as he was, Tate chose to have a small fire. He knew the Indians would not be smelling his smoke with so many cook fires of their own going as they feasted on the fresh buffalo kill, but he took precautions anyway. Choosing only the driest wood, making a small hat-sized fire with stones stacked around, and placing it under the outspread branches of the big ponderosa to disperse the smoke, he felt confident he could cook his supper and boil his coffee without giving away his location. With potatoes and onion roasting in the coals and the fresh sheep steaks hanging over the flame, his dinner was ready in just a short while. The pup was lying beside him and watching the steaks drip onto the flames and quickly turned his head and let a low growl rumble. Tate looked at the pup and quietly said, "It's O.K., boy, I heard 'em." Then he lifted his voice and said, "Welcome to my fire. There's meat to share if you're hungry." He nonchalantly reached for a willow withe that held a sizzling steak and leaned back against the large stone at fire's edge.

He turned to see three Indian warriors, thinking they were probably Arapaho as Knuckles had warned, and motioned to them to take a steak. They stood unmoving until Little Raven, using sign language, asked why the white man was here. Tate had learned sign language from the Kiowa, Comanche, and Knuckles, and readily responded that he was traveling through the country going to the south end of the mountains.

The three warriors looked around his camp without moving from their place. Each one showed a readiness to fight with hands on knives or tomahawks, quivers that held unstrung bows and many arrows, and a countenance that showed no trust. Tate dropped his hand to the head of Lobo to keep him still and the move was seen by Little Raven. The man spoke in Arapaho as he used the signs, asking about the wolf. Tate explained he was left after he and his friend had killed the pack when they attacked the mustangs and their horses. Tate stroked the head of the wolf, now standing and watching each of the warriors, appearing as if he was ready to attack.

Little Raven told Tate his name, asked for his and Tate made the sign of Longbow. Little Raven then surprised Tate by asking in English, "What is your white man name?"

"Tate Saint, but I am known by native peoples as Longbow."

"What people gave you that name?" asked Little Raven.

"I was given that name by chief Dohäsan of the Kiowa. But I am known by that name among the Comanche, Apache, Crow, and now by you of the Arapaho."

Little Raven looked at this white man with skepticism, then said, "You have come in peace, you may go in peace." Tate watched the three warriors as they turned and walked away from the camp, and let a long sigh escape and his shoulders slump as he relaxed. He patted Lobo on the head, and the pup dropped to his belly as Tate offered him a scrap from his steak.

Tate resumed his practice of traveling at night and departed his camp during the time just after twilight and before the moon rose to share its light. He crossed the creek in the bottom of the valley, moved beyond the willows to the tree line of spruce and fir, and soon located a game trail well obscured with the trees. Lobo, now riding behind the cantle and draped over the rump of Shady, bobbed his head with the gait of the horse. The line of four horses moved silently along the trail with an abundance of pine needles that quieted their passing, and soon moved beyond the camp of the Arapaho. The moon, now waxing toward full, rose and gave a beacon before Tateas the pass he sought crossed the natural saddle of the mountains.

He moved at a leisurely pace, giving the grulla his head and letting him amble along. The trail was a constant climb until about midnight, when the trees, now mostly bristlecone pine with a few fir, gave way to reveal a tundra covered meadow with an abundance of interlaced ponds. Tate reined up and watched a big nosed moose, standing knee deep in one of the ponds with greenery hanging from his mouth, look over his domain. This massive animal, with antlers that Tate calculated to have a width of twice the length of his Hawken, was an unusual sight in these mountains. Tate had never seen one before and had never heard the old mountain men to speak of them. He watched as the bull dropped his head into the water again, brought up another mouthful of tender greens and continue to munch on his dinner. After a few moments, Tate gigged his mount forward and they soon crested the pass.

As they stood in the open, Tate could see through the cut of the mountains, the valley below framed on both sides by towering peaks. He sucked in the mountain air, stood in his stirrups for a better look-see and dropped into his saddle. He kneed the grulla and soon found a trail on the low side of the shoulder of the mountains to his left. The moon hung high above, shedding its light across the black trees and the grey mountains with spots of white showing the pockets of snow still held in the higher elevation. He looked through the trees to see the winding stream in the bottom, chuckling its way over the rocks and twisting through the formations as it wound lower on the mountains. They rounded a bend in the trail and high above rose pillared cliffs of light grey, spot-lighted by the big moon, making the formations appear as a legion of ghosts standing guard over the mountain pass. The shadows moved as the travelers passed and the moon followed its arc of the night.

With the ridge to his left rising sharply above him, he chose to cross over the stream in the bottom, what he now thought to be the headwaters of the Wind River and move into the thicker black trees along the low sloping hillside. It was nearing sunrise and he wanted to be camped before the light of morning. The winding stream had ample grass covering the flats nearby and leading up to the edge of the trees. Tate soon found a suitable campsite tucked away in the pines and straddling a spring fed creek that was no more than one pace wide. He waited until full light before building a coffee-making fire, and with belly full and horses grazing but sheltered in the trees, he stretched out, Lobo at his side, for his morning snooze.

The gunshot echoed through the valley and instantly brought Tate from his snooze. He sat up, grabbing his Hawken as he did, and searched the trees for any sign of attack. The pup stood with front feet on Tate's leg, looking around for the source of disturbance. Tate looked at the horses, hobbled at the edge of the clearing. All were standing stock still, looking down the valley, ears forward. Tate slowly stood, slipped his powder horn and possibles bag over his head, strapped on his belt with the holstered Paterson and slipped the Bowie into the sheath at his back. In the distance, he heard voices, and thought both the gunshot and voices came from the same location. He started into the trees, stealthily making his way toward the sounds.

The voices had stilled, but Tate smelled the smoke of a cookfire and the scent of frying meat. Using the pine needles to muffle any sounds, he cautiously made his way through the trees, Lobo at his heels, and neared the camp of the noisemakers. Staying well back in the shadows but near enough to glimpse the activity of the camp and hear the people, he waited and watched. Occasionally he would move to one side or the other as he surveyed the camp. Noting three horses tethered away from the clearing, he also noted two saddles and a pack saddle in the camp. That told of two men with one pack animal. As he watched, he saw two scruffy looking white men, both unshaven and attired in buckskins, lounging against a log and talking. An Indian woman was working at the fire, cooking the meal for the men.

Tate worked a little closer to hear some of the conversation, he bellied down and slowly crawled, staying in the dark shadows and behind the larger ponderosa.

"Wal, when 'er we gonna meet up with Jacques and Thumbs?" asked the smaller of the men.

"How should I know, he said we was to meet him at the beginnin' o' Union Pass and to get thar 'n wait. Way he figgered it, should be sometime in this comin' week. He said it'd take them missionaries a bit longer, but we was to wait anyhoo. Don't know what'chur belly achin' 'bout anyways, now we got us a woman, whut's the hurry?" said the other man, elbowing his friend and cackling.

"What'chu mean, we? You wouldn't let me near her las' night! An' all you did was snuggle up after she went ta' sleep."

"Look Snake, I tol' you we gotta tame 'er slow. Cain't just go forcin' her. We do that'n she won't cook fer us. Now, fer's I'm concerned, I like her cookin' better'n yourn!" snarled the big man, rubbing his belly.

"I ain't inters'ted in her cookin', I want sum comp'ny!" whined the one named Snake.

The woman bent over the frying pan, and Snake grabbed at his knee, and within an instant, he snapped a black-snake bullwhip that slapped the posterior of the woman, making her stand upright and grab at the whip. Snake had brought it back and cackled at the reaction of the woman, who stood glaring at the little man.

"Now, that's how ya' tame a squaw!" declared Snake.

The bigger man laughed and cautioned, "Mebbe so, but don't get too careless wit' that thang, you could cut that buckskin dress right off'a her!"

"Now, thar's an idee!" snapped Snake and stood coiling up

the bullwhip and readying another strike.

As the whip whistled behind the man, Tate snatched it from the air and jerked it out of the man's hands. He dropped it to the ground, lifted his Hawken, and said, "That ain't no way to treat a woman!" His sudden appearance and the sound of his voice masked the click of cocking the hammer and setting his trigger. He stood at a casual stance, Hawken cradled in his left arm but pointing in the general direction of the men's camp. The whip wielder snarled, "Gimme my whip!" but Tate ignored him choosing to watch the big man reach for his rifle, and warned, "Don't do it!" but the man did not heed the warning and grabbed his rifle as he started to stand and turn. Tate hesitated just long enough to know the man was going to try to bring his rifle to bear and Tate squeezed the trigger, taking his shot from his hip. The .54 caliber ball caught the man just left of his breast bone and carried him back off his feet to land just inches from the fire. The little man looked at his partner, back at Tate and whined, "Now, you had no call to do that! You kilt him!"

"No, he did that all by his ownself. I told him not to, but stubborn is as stubborn does!" declared Tate. The little man looked around, realizing Tate had fired his only shot, grinned and reached for his own rifle, but when he looked back at Tate, he was shocked to be staring down the barrel of the Colt Paterson, making him freeze in his movements.

"Uh, uh, now hold on mister, I ain't gonna do nuthin', honest!"

"Then drop that rifle right where you stand and back away." Tate watched Snake move back and he looked at the woman. He was surprised to see she was young and quite attractive. Her knee length buckskin dress had little bead-work, but fringe at the bottom edge and along the short sleeves. He looked at her and asked, "Do you speak English?"

She nodded her head and said, "Some, yes."

"How long have you been with these men?"

"They took me one day."

He looked back at the whiner and said, "You took her? From where?"

"Her people were busy with a buffalo jump an' we seen her in the woods, pickin' berries, so we took her," explained the man, shifting his weight from one foot to the other, acting like a child anxious to go to the outhouse.

Tate looked at the girl again and asked her name and was told White Fawn.

"Well, White Fawn, I'm thinkin' you could probably find your way back to your people easy enough, so why don't you take that man's horse," motioning to the dead man, "and just skedaddle on home."

"You mean I can go?

He nodded his head and said, "Yup, oh, and tell Little Raven thanks!"

The girl looked surprised as she slowly walked to the tethered horses. After retrieving the black horse and leading it back to saddle it, she looked again at this young white man and asked, "You know Little Raven?"

"Well, let's just say I met him the other day," explained Tate.

"Little Raven is my brother, I will tell him of you."

"So, why hasn't your brother come after you?" asked Tate.

"There was much to do with the buffalo, and I go away by myself. They do not know I am gone," she explained.

He looked at the girl, thought again how pretty she was, and watched as she saddled the horse. Although the saddles made by the Indians are quite different, she had no difficulty with the more cumbersome saddle of the dead man. She mounted up, looked at Tate and smiled, asked, "We will see you again?"

"Maybe so, maybe so. I'd like that."

She smiled at his response, said, "I am grateful," and kneed the horse to trot away and soon disappeared into the trees.

Tate turned his attention on the sniveling man and said, "Now, what am I gonna do with you?"

"Let me go?" whined the man.

Tate thought for a moment, stepped to the edge of the trees and looked down the valley, motioned for the man to come closer and pointed down the valley to a point well over two miles distant. "See where that ridge sticks out into the valley a bit?" motioning downstream. The little man craned his neck and said, "Yeah, what of it?"

"Here's what I'm gonna do. I'm gonna take your horse," and was interrupted by the whiner, "You cain't leave me afoot! I'll die in this country!"

"Shut up and listen! Now, I'm gonna take your horse and your rifle and I'll leave 'em somewhere at the tree line just around that point. That'll give me plenty of time to be long gone and you won't be afoot. Now, if I ever see you again, and if you're up to no good, then you better make things right with your Maker, cuz I'll be sending you to meet Him. Understand?"

"Oh, yessir, yessir. You leave me muh horse and rifle an' I'll be grateful, yessir. I'll plum skedaddle outta this country fer good, yessir!"

"Well, we'll see about that. Now, back up to that tree yonder, I'm gonna tie your hands together, but it won't take you too long to get free, just make sure I'm long gone 'fore you try, understand?"

"Yessir, yessir. What e'er you say. And I'ma thankin' you, I am. Shore don't wanna join muh friend yonder," nodding to the body of the big man.

"Well, it'll be up to you to put him under," stated Tate, and finished with, "Don't go tryin' to tame any more women either. I'm takin' that whip of yours."

CHAPTER ELEVEN
BREAKDOWN

"I'M TELLIN' YA, I GOT IT FIGGERED OUT. I WORKED ON THAT axle so it'll give out an' it'll take 'em at least a day, mebbe as many as two, three, mebbe e'en four days to git 'er fixed. Them missionaries'll be so anxious, they'll foller anybody," growled Jacques as he spoke to his sidekick, Thumbs. They were riding far ahead of the wagon train, hunting for meat and scouting for Indians or other dangers. "I tol' Snake n' Roscoe to meet us whar the Union Pass leaves the valley an' we can do 'em in right thar. That last wagon, the one wit' the girl, has the money box and what with the money an' anything else they got, we can cut fer Californy an' be livin' high on the hog long fer anybody finds 'em. And e'en then, we'll make it look like injuns done it!"

"Can we take that girl wit' us?" grinned Thumbs.

"What fer?" asked Jacques. "Anybody find us wit' her, she'd tell 'em what happened and then our goose'd be cooked!"

"Yeah, but in the meantime . . . " cackled Thumbs. "Hey, mebbe e'erbody'd think the injuns took her!" exclaimed the lecherous reprobate.

"We'll see when we get thar," considered Jacques, "but right now, we'uns need some meat!"

THE WAGON TRAIN was on schedule, at least as far as estimated by Sublette. They had followed the North Platte for the last six days and had followed the bend of the river to the south just this morning. The only green on the route was that along the North Platte, any distance away from the river bottom yielded nothing but sagebrush, cactus and bunch grass. It was a desolate land that promised nothing but hardship.

For the past week, Narcissa had suspected someone had spoken to Jacques about her reservations concerning the two scouts. They had been extra attentive the past several days, always on their best behavior, constantly providing the missionaries with fresh meat, and being very mannerly in their conversation, even going so far as to keep them informed as to their whereabouts and what the road ahead promised. One of their discussions was about the possibility of a short-cut to the north that could save them some time. Reverend Spalding had listened attentively and after the two men left, he went to Sublette and discussed the alternate route. Sublette agreed there was another way, although not an often traveled one, that could possibly save them as much as a week or more, but that route would require them leaving the train when the North Platte turned south. Narcissa was thinking about that as the train followed the wide loop of the big river and was pointed south, just as the sun rested on the western horizon and painted the sky with a blaze of oranges and reds. They usually traveled at least another few miles, but for some reason, this time they made camp a little early.

As usual, when the meal was just about ready, Eliza whispered to Narcissa, "Here he comes. Don't know what he's gonna do when he has to go back to eating with the rest of the men." Narcissa grinned at her friend and looked up to see Sublette hobbling to their fire with his solitary crutch aiding his walk. The cork leg was still new to him and he was struggling a bit getting used to it, but he had been told he should eventually be able to maneuver with nothing more than a cane. "Evenin' ladies! Whatever it is you're fixin' sure smells good. I could have found my way here with my eyes closed, it smells so good."

"Ah, go on with you now, a flattering tongue will get you nowhere with us, Mr. Sublette. Come on and have a seat, it'll be ready right soon," declared Eliza, grinning at their company.

As Narcissa stirred the pot hanging from the tripod and suspended over the fire. She looked at their guest and asked, "Didn't we stop a little early this evening?"

"Yes'm, we did. One of our wagons was havin' a bit of trouble and when we pulled up, the front axle split plum in two. It's gonna take some time to get it fixed. Not sure how long it'll be, we carry a few spare parts, but axles just don't break that often, so we don't have a spare. Each of the wagons're loaded heavy an' I'm not sure we'll be able to offload that'n and I dunno it the men'll be able to fix it. But I got a good man workin' on it. If he can't fix it, it can't be fixed."

The Reverend Spalding and Marcus Whitman and the other men had joined the group at the fire and had listened to the explanation. Reverend Spalding asked, "The other day when we spoke about that shortcut, wasn't it about here that you said we would have to take it?"

"Yessir, anywhere along here. If we go much farther south, like the train is goin' to hit the Sweetwater, you'll lose a day. Is that what you're thinkin' 'bout doin'?"

"We considered it but weren't too sure. However, now

that you say we might have to wait a few days for the wagon to be fixed, that's a different story altogether. It's something we'll have to think and pray about," somberly stated the reverend.

"If we were to do that, Mr. Sublette, we need your honest opinion about Jacques and Thumbs. Are they really trustworthy? I mean, not just to know the country, but can we depend on them to get us there?" asked Marcus.

"Well, Mr. Whitman, as I've said before, I ain't known these men long, but they have shown themselves to be dependable to do the job they were hired for, and they've been resourceful. Now, as to their crude ways, most of that comes from spending most of their lives in the mountains with other hard men ekeing out a living where many men die. But most men in the west are very respectful of women, leastways white women, and are careful to protect them and respect them. I will say I've known many mountain men, traded with 'em, fought beside 'em, even lived with 'em, and there's not a group of men I'd rather have beside me if the chips were down."

"But as far as these two men are concerned, have you known them to be less than trustworthy? Or have you heard of anyone that knew them to be less than trustworthy?" asked the Reverend.

"I've been to many rendezvous and I do not remember any dealings with them or any stories, good or bad, about them. But, you must understand, at any rendezvous, there are as many as two or three thousand people there, including the Indians, and it is difficult to know each and every one. But, most men of the mountains know the reputations of those that are very good and also those that are very bad. But again, I have heard nothing either way about these men. If I had, known anything bad about them, they would not be in my employ."

The conversation of the men was interrupted by Eliza's announcement that dinner was ready, and the group quickly gathered at the plank board table, taking seats on barrels and boxes, to make ready for the evening feast. When it was over, and Sublette excused himself, the men and women gathered together to discuss their plans. Each one shared their concerns and reservations, each was discussed at length and finally the Reverend said, "Let's join hands and pray together, seek God's will, and then make our decision." The Amen was no sooner said than a voice came from beside the wagon, "Uh, folks, uh, Mr. Sublette sent me down hyar to talk wit' you folks. He said y'all was a thinkin' 'bout takin' that short cut. Am I right?"

It was Jacques and Thumbs that stood beside the wagon, hats in hand. They stepped into the light and gave a rather timid appearance. Marcus motioned for them to take a seat and the Reverend said, "Yes, but first we have a few questions, if you don't mind."

The men took a seat on a couple of upended crates and pulled up to the plank table. The Reverend began, "First, we'd like to know about this route you speak of, have you traveled it before?"

"Uh, yessir. The way I figger on goin' is up the Wind an' take the Union Pass o'er the mountains. That'd drop us off near the headwaters o' th' Green. Thar's 'nother river, got no name, we'd foller up to the Snake, 'n go north from thar," explained Jacques.

"And how long do you think it will take?"

"Wal, wit' th' wagons, it'd be a mite slower'n horses, o'course, but from here to that thar lake would be two weeks, mebbe a little longer. That'd be 'bout half-way to the Nez Perce country, so we be lookin' at 'bout a month, give 'er take."

The group looked from one to the other and each was

thinking that would be almost two weeks less than the original route was thought to be, giving them much more time to prepare for the coming winter. A look of relief seemed to be contagious as the group nodded to one another. The Reverend then asked, "And how much to you expect to be paid for this?"

Jacques took on a serious look and thought a moment, looked at his partner, then looked to the Reverend and said, "Well, we was thinkin' if you'ns paid us the same whut we're gittin' now with Sublette, that'd be fine with us."

"And what is he paying you?" asked Marcus.

"Well sir, he'sa payin' us thirty dollar a month. Each."

Marcus looked to the Reverend who nodded his head and turned to Mrs. Price with a wave of the hand, sending her to get the money. Jacques realized what they were doing, and he spoke up, "Oh, no sir. We don't want th' money now. No, sir. 'Sides, ain't no place to spend it. You just hang on to it till we gits thar. Then you can pay us. That'd be fine with us."

Thumbs looked at his partner with a bit of a scowl, shrugged his shoulders and nodded his head in agreement. The missionaries were pleased with this, thinking the men were not just after some money after all. All the men stood, and the Reverend extended his hand and said, "Then we have agreement. I expect we'll leave at first light?"

Jacques started shaking hands with each of the men and agreed, "Yessir, first light."

When the two scouts left the circle, the missionaries chatted a few moments and turned in, knowing dawn would come early and there was much to do before leaving. All seemed to be excited and anxious to start this part of their journey. Unknown to them, the two scouts walked away from the group to their separate camp and Thumbs asked in a whisper, "Why didn't you take the money?"

Jacques looked at his partner and answered in a low voice, "Why take a little now? When we can jes' wait till the right time an' take it all! And more 'sides!"

CHAPTER TWELVE
LOOKOUT

TATE WAS A THINKER. FROM THE TIME HIS FATHER FIRST introduced him to the adventures found in books, he would lose himself in those pages and become one with the characters, often trying to soak up all the qualities of the heroes and mimic them in his own life. His dad spent many hours in the tutelage of his son, always working to instill the qualities of good character and sound judgment. These moments of solitude lent to reflection and introspection and he was bothered by the recent events. He had never killed a white man, and even though he knew he was not given a choice, it still bothered him. But why? He realized he was rationalizing that there was a difference between a white man and an Indian, and he also realized how wrong that was, because life was the same no matter the image it took. His father had often said, "Son, when you consider people, you must look at their character, and the color of their skin has nothing to do with character."

A man's behavior and treatment of others would always reveal the quality of character in a man. Anyone that took advantage of others or treated them with anything less than respect, told a great deal about that person's temperament. Sadly, too many times in this wilderness, any vestige of character that a man had was often buried under necessities for survival. But true character cannot remain buried under any circumstances. It is the lack of character and its companion, morals, that make a man what he is, but all too often others judge a man by his possessions, position, appearance or power, believing these things are gained by good works and sound judgment. His father had taught Tate that things do not make a man, but circumstances will reveal a man, and time will always test the metal and character of a true man. And Tate had seen that first hand after his father was killed. The community leaders showed their values and character when they told Tate to leave their home before his father's body was even in the ground. They were more concerned about the next teacher, than the welfare of a young man. It was a bitter lesson to learn, but one that became a building block of Tate's judgment of others.

He thought of the two men that had taken the Arapaho woman captive. They were typical of those that refused to work for what they needed and thought they could just take what they wanted, others were there for their convenience and pleasure. Throughout history there were always those that tried to set themselves above others, or to tear down those that were above them. But God had always put good men where they were needed, men that were willing to put others above themselves, and to seek the best for those around them. That was the kind of men that would build a great nation, that was the kind of man Tate aspired to become.

What he had done to free the young Arapaho woman was nothing more than necessary, the right thing to do at the time as he had been taught. But he remembered the conversation the men had before he confronted them. It was something about an intended meeting with two others and some missionaries, and the way they talked, it certainly wasn't to attend a Bible lesson. *It was something about Union Pass, that must be a pass that would take them over the Wind River mountains,* mused Tate as he looked at the long range of granite peaks that held patches of snow.

He rounded the tip of the ridge he pointed out from the camp of the two men and began searching for a good place to tether the horses. This was about two and a half miles from their camp and out of sight of the wide river bottomed flat. But if the man known as Snake followed directions, he could easily find the chosen tether point. Tate stretched a picket line between two spruce trees, giving the horses ample graze and water from the nearby feeder creek. He dropped the saddle and pack saddles under a nearby tree and checked the tethers, ensuring they were tight enough so the horses would know they were tied, but loose enough so that if necessary they could free themselves. He was more concerned with the horses than he was for the sniveling degenerate called Snake.

Satisfied with his work, he mounted up and moved out to cross the river and find a trail in the darker timber on the east facing slope of the mountain range. As they moved along the narrow trail, winding its way through the rocky outcroppings and thick timber, avoiding the downfall of the many trees that creaked in the wind, he thought, wondered, and considered. With no maps of the west, men depended on the experiences of others. Whenever men of the mountains gathered, they shared information about trails traveled, sights seen, travails survived. Always making mental notes of landmarks, trails, mountain passes, and campsites and shelters, for these shared tidbits could save a life someday. Many of those places were given names based on what they had seen, names like Ratttlesnake gulch, Crazy Woman creek, Poison Spider Flats; names that told of first impressions. Tate began to remember shared tales with the mountain men on the riverboat, stories told by Knuckles, and wisdom garnered from Indians and others. He searched his mind for trails and passes of the Wind River range. *If they're waiting for some missionaries, they're probably in wagons, and they mentioned Union Pass. Now if there's a pass that cuts through these mountains, I'm bound to run into it sooner or later. But then what? I don't know when they're coming, don't know when the troublemakers are gonna attack, or what they're gonna do, and I sure don't know where they're gonna do it. Maybe I'll just have to do what Pa always said, 'Whenever you have a problem, just think it through one step at a time, kinda take it apart and study it, then work out your best solution and get with it!' So, I guess my first step is to find the pass.*

The shadows stretched off the slope, reaching for the flats below. The side slope stretched to the top of a shoulder bluff with fir, spruce, and pines crowding each other for tenuous toe holds in the rocky soil. The trail twisted through a wide swath of aspen and then a wide trail cut across the narrow game trail he was following. It showed sign of a few wagons having made the trek before the winter just past, but it was a rough roadway, nothing for greenhorns to attempt. Tate reined his mount to the middle of the wide trail, stood in his stirrups to look up the hill, but could only see as far as a switchback in the roadway. He looked below and saw the cut in the timber that marked the beginning of the road as it led from the flats. He reined the grulla to go uphill and follow the roadway.

He started uphill, made the cutback and found the trail to sidle along the face of the timber covered hill. At the south edge, the trail bent around the ridge and broke into a bald face of the hillside. He looked back to his right and up the slope to a peak he guessed would hold a good promontory to overlook the valley and the beginning of Union Pass.

Nearing the crest of the hill, he noted a shoulder that held a smattering of skinny fir trees and a good flat of grass. He heard the trickle of a small stream and knew he had found his campsite.

Once settled in, he stood, stretched and watched the rising moon. The big full orb shined like a lamplight and gave the terrain a muted glow with irregular shadows. His promontory gave him a view unparalleled anywhere. In the distance to the east rose the needles of the Absaroka range, and farther still were the shadows that whispered of another mountain range. Below him snaked the Wind River with the reflection of the white shining moon showing the twisting river as a silver thread winding through the willows and alders to make its way through a cut just downstream. But further still, the valley opened up and the crystalline snake hid its secrets and carried them away beyond the sight of the night. It was a beautiful but wild country, and Tate felt right at home. These mountains held him like the cradle of a new born and helpless infant, giving boundaries but holding promises beyond his imagination.

He lingered at the edge of his campsite, looking at the outcropping of rock that hung from the pyramid shaped hill like a handle on a massive crock. It would give him an unobscured view of the roadway leading up the valley, and with the aid of his telescope, he could see any wagons or other travelers long before they reached the crossing of the Wind River that would begin the ascent of Union Pass. *I just hope I'm in time and that I can keep them missionaries from getting waylaid by these hombres. Well, no sense in borrowin' trouble 'fore it comes. Like Pa said, 'One step at a time, boy, one step at a time.'*

He rolled out of his blankets before the first light of dawn crested the mountains in the east, and with Lobo at his side, he gathered the fixings for his morning coffee and breakfast. He rummaged through the panniers for his utensils and pan and coffeepot, fetched the water for his coffee and readied everything for his first meal of the day. He waited until the long rays of the morning sun pierced the black timber, giving light enough to prevent a small fire from betraying his presence. Within a short while he was sitting back against the big boulder, sipping his coffee and eating the broiled steak from the sheep and the few onions he baked in the coals. He was pleased with his choice and when finished, set the plate aside and savored the coffee. He looked around his camp, thinking about what he would do to productively use his time and decided to begin the tanning process on the sheepskin. He knew the leather from the bighorn would be lighter and softer than buckskin but just as durable. The Indians would often use the softer leather for dancing tunics and special events, decorating it more elaborately than other clothing items. He wasn't interested in decorating, but the softer leather was appealing, although he wasn't sure what he would use it for, first he had to get it tanned. He had done some tanning, but most of the leather goods he had were from hides tanned by White Feather of the Comanche. He had watched her scrape and treat the hides, and had learned a lot from her, but this would be the first time he did it on his own, since he left the Comanche some time ago. But he could not allow his tanning to interfere with his lookout as he waited for the wagons.

He walked out to the promontory, Lobo following, his telescope in hand. He dropped to a crouch and slowly moved nearer the edge. As he approached, he bellied down and chuckled when Lobo copied his moves, dropping to his belly and dragging himself beside Tate. Once at the edge, he looked both upstream and down, the put the glass to his eye and began a more thorough survey. He followed the road, more of a trail than a road, down the valley. The valley narrowed just below the hillside but widened again beyond the cut. He could see for a distance he estimated at three to four miles, and nothing moved. He turned to look just below the hillside and followed the winding river upstream, moving side to side to view the wider valley, searching for any trails along the lower hillsides. He saw several deer, two elk, a shadow that he thought was a black bear, as he continued slowly looking over the dell. This was the valley he followed on the trail that was tucked back in the timber, but there were other easier trails, game trails, that snaked along the flats. He had looked well up the riverbottom and was just about to take the glass down when he saw movement. His first thought was of more elk or even a grizzly, but he then nothing. He rested the long tube of the telescope on a rock, moved to a more comfortable position, and slowly scanned the upper end of the vale. There, the movement again, just past the cluster of alder near the stream. Then stepping out from behind the brush came two horses, one with a packsaddle and the other carrying a man. But the distance was too far to identify the man, but there was something familiar about the figure.

Tate watched the creatures in the distance, moving at an easy walk, and waited. As he looked, he became certain the only man that could be was Snake. He had found his horses and was moving down the valley. He had said he was going to leave, and this was the easiest way for him to travel to leave the mountains, but Tate didn't believe him when he said it, and didn't believe he was leaving now. The overheard conversation told of meeting his other partners at the beginning of Union Pass, and that was just below Tate's promontory. *Well, we'll just see where that Snake slithers to, won't we? If he's like the snake I think he is, he'll crawl behind those rocks and wait for his friends to show.*

CHAPTER THIRTEEN
TRAVEL

SINCE SEPARATING FROM THE FUR TRAPPERS CARAVAN AND THE company of William Sublette, the travel of the four wagons and missionaries had been pleasant, almost enjoyable. Narcissa had commented about the apparent change in the countenance of Jacques and Thumbs and was pleased to share their provided bounty of antelope, mule deer, and jackrabbits, with the two men who were often invited to supper. Jacques seemed to remember his manners and the better part of his upbringing, but the same could not be said for Thumbs. The smaller man was often too anxious to eat to wait for the prayer of Marcus Whitman. But with Jacques occasionally slapping the grabby hands of Thumbs during the asking of the blessing, the uncouth mountain man's manners had shown an improvement.

Even the after-dinner conversations had become pleasant, with Marcus repeatedly speaking from the scriptures and sharing the Biblical truths with the two men. Narcissa was certain that Jacques' patience was wearing thin, but the two men apparently saw the good meals and the conversations as a trade-off and they continued to enjoy the former.

The journey was not without its difficulties, powdery dust that choked both beast and man and brackish water that caused them to deplete their supplies had caused tempers to flare and patience to wear thin. Marcus would often take his saddle horse and explore the rock formations that seemed to rise from the sandy soil at the edge of the many bluffs. He had referred to the formations as the bastions of the sand castles of the desert, and seeing the pillars of stone he thought they were indeed a marvel to behold. But even the most amazing geologic features held hazards and Marcus had been a witness to what he whispered to his wife was a disciplinary chastisement from the Lord upon Thumbs. The cantankerous mountain man was trying to flush any game out of the many cuts, ravines, and small gorges that marked the rim-rock bluffs and of a sudden his horse took to the air, twisted completely around and came down facing the opposite direction, much to the alarm of the rider who jerked on reins and dug in his heels, which just exasperated the already frightened horse who had made the initial jump to escape an angry rattlesnake. With the snake coiled and threatening to strike, the rider was vociferously chastising, striking and kicking the animal. The horse reared up, dropped his front feet into the dust alongside his nose that blew snot bubbles in the dust, kicked at the lone cloud in the sky and then defied gravity and reason by launching himself into the air, twisting in the middle and showed his belly to the sun. This caused the man to find himself making a vain attempt at flying without wings, before the horse came down on all fours and disappeared in a dust cloud.

Marcus was near enough to see the entire show but far enough away, so his horse was not alarmed, and the missionary could not stop himself from laughing at the antics of man and beast. When the dust cleared, and Thumbs found his feet, he started shaking his fist at the fleeing horse, making threats of any manner of death as he spit dirt from his mouth. He laid a finger aside of his nose and let loose with a gob of snot that would make a domestic swine envious. Marcus sat on his mount, watching the display of disappointment and disgrace, and laughed. When Thumbs heard the laughter, he wiped dust from his face and eyes to see the missionary having a hoot at his expense, and he shook his fist at the man, threatening, "You'll getchurs soon e'nuff, then we'll see who's laughin'!"

Marcus just thought the man meant that with everything that happens on a trip such as this, everyone was bound to have his moment. He kneed his mount forward and kicked his foot free of a stirrup and said, "Climb on, we'll see if we can catch that crazy cayuse, as you called him."

Thumbs looked up at him, let a grunt of dismay escape, but gave a slight hop and planted his foot in the stirrup to swing up behind Marcus. When his passenger was settled, Marcus kneed his horse in the direction of the fleeing mount and the two men rode without a word. They soon came upon the now docile horse, munching on bunchgrass.

NARCISSA HAD BECOME adept at handling the four-up hitch of mules and it was not unusual for her to be at the lines, sitting on the spring seat, shaded by the canvas bonnet, and letting the mules have their head as they followed the wagon driven by the Reverend Spalding. Eliza would usually join Narcissa when she was at the reins, giving the women some special time together away from the men. She spoke to Narcissa, "Well, I don't care what the men think. You can't change a leopard's spots, not that I've ever seen one, but you know what I mean. I still think both those men are reprehensible and I long for and pray for the day when we'll be rid of them." She nodded her head and crossed her arms across her chest to emphasize her remarks.

"Well, what makes you so certain, Eliza?" asked Narcissa, looking at her friend.

"Haven't you noticed? That little one, especially, whenever he thinks no one is looking he practically leers at me, and you too! He has even gone so far as to lick his lips and nod his head, like he was looking at candy in a canister on the counter. It just makes me uncomfortable! And when I mention it to Henry, he just shakes his head and makes excuses for the man."

"Well, let's do our best to avoid them, both of them," declared Narcissa. "But, when our husbands ask them to dinner, we'll just have to keep our distance."

"Speaking of keeping a distance, why don't the Prices ever come to dinner with us?" asked Eliza. "She is so quiet, I don't think she's said but a handful of words to me. What about you?"

"No, she's definitely not a conversationalist, but as for dinner, have you ever invited her?" responded Narcissa, casting Eliza a sidelong glance.

"Uh, yes, yes I did. But it's been some time now, they just keep to themselves, mostly. I think she's concerned about that young daughter of hers. That girl is, well, sometimes I think she's just shameless, the way she looks at men. Not so much now that we've left the other wagons, but while we were with them, she was always smiling at any man that passed by."

"Now, Eliza, it wasn't that bad. She was just being friendly. There's no one her age for her to be friends with, and I imagine she gets lonely," explained Narcissa. "Maybe what we should do is make it a point to invite the family to join us for supper, how about tonight? If you're willing, as soon as we stop, I'll go back to their wagon and ask them to join us. After all, Reverend Spalding trusts Mrs. Price to manage the books and take care of the money for the Mission, at least we should be better acquainted. I just imagine that Amy needs a friend. Don't you think?"

Eliza had fashioned herself a fan from a thin slab of bark and now put her handiwork to the test as she fanned the dust from their faces. A sudden drop of a wheel into a slight depression startled them and brought a short exclamation of surprise from them both, causing the two women to break into laughter as they looked at the dusty faces of one another. At the sight of her friend's dirty face, Narcissa said, "Oh, I hope we have plenty of water when we camp this evening."

She had no sooner mentioned water when the wagon before her dropped over the edge of the bluff and disappeared below the rise. As their team crested the edge, they were afforded a view of a white-water river with green banks of grass and willows. The women gasped at the sight, looked to one another and smiled and said together, "Finally!" Before them was the narrow valley of the Wind River, as promised by Jacques. When their wagon reached the level greenery, Jacques rode alongside and said, "Ladies, I laid a antelope carcass o'er yore tailgate. Should make good eatin' fer ya' tonite! Oh, an' we'll cross o'er the river 'fore we stop, so just keep 'em movin' an' we'll stop on th' other side and fill up our water barrels an' such."

"Thank you, Jacques! We appreciate the meat!" called Narcissa to the back of Jacques as he rode up alongside the wagon driven by Reverend Spalding. He waved at the ladies and began to speak with the Reverend, motioning to the river and giving instructions about crossing. With scarcely a pause, the Spalding wagon started down the slight incline of the rocky ramp into the water with the mules stepping into the swift stream. Narcissa reined up on her mules, looked around, stood on the seat to look over the bonnet behind the wagon, frantically trying to locate her husband. She was frightened at the idea of trying to cross the river. As she looked, she heard a shout from the river, and watched as the current began to push the wagon, causing it to bounce along the rocky riverbed. The Reverend was shouting, slapping reins to the mules, and she saw him grab a small stone from the seat and throw it at the lead pair of mules. With continued shouting and creaking of wheels and the twisting of the bed of the wagon, the splashing of water against the sideboards, and the uncertain movements, Narcissa was frightened for the Reverend Spalding and the wagon. With the river being no more than about twenty yards wide, the mules had found solid footing and were leaning into the traces to pull the wagon out of the strong current and into the shallows to rise from the water on the low bank.

Narcissa dropped into the seat, let a heavy sigh escape and looked at her friend, and said, "I don't think I can do it! Where is that man?" she almost shouted as she searched for Marcus. Suddenly, beside the wagon came an answer, "I'm right here woman, don't go gettin' so upset. Now, how 'bout you women climbin' in the back an' let me take the lines, unless of course you'd rather ride the horse across."

"Oh, you, I was ready to wring your neck! No, I don't want to ride the horse, you just tie him on back and he can follow," she instructed as she followed Eliza into the back of the wagon. Marcus climbed aboard and took the lines, slapped them on the rumps of the mules and hollered, "Heeeyaahhhh, let's go mules, let's go!" The big mules leaned into their harness and pulled the trace chains taut and the wagon creaked in protest as it followed.

The crossing of the second wagon was uneventful. The current did not lift nor move the wagon and the mules kept a steady pull and the wagon was soon on dry ground on the far bank. Marcus looked at the women and as he started to climb down, stepping down on the wheel and the hub, he listened to the questioning of his wife, "That was easier than I expected. Why didn't our wagon bounce and slide with the current like the Reverend's?"

Marcus grinned and motioned with his hand toward his wife and her friend and answered mischievously, "Uh, ladies, we had more weight on board!" He quickly ducked as his wife swung an open hand toward his grinning face, but he stepped down and she missed. She answered, "That's because I've been feeding my husband so well, but maybe it's time he had his rations cut!"

With ample daylight left the women convinced Jacques to make an early stop and allow them time for washing some clothes and bathing. He agreed and the women: Narcissa, Eliza, Amy and Melissa quickly gathered the clothes and soaps and trotted upstream to a bend in the river that afforded a backwater pool above a rocky expanse with plenty of scrubbing stones. The men had divided responsibilities with Marcus and Jacques going on a hunt downstream toward the opening of the river canyon and the Reverend, Nathan Price, and William Gray, busy with a thorough greasing of the wagon wheel hubs and a general check of the rest.

This was the first time in several weeks the women were afforded the opportunity for washing and bathing. Sublette had planned just such a stop, but the separation of the groups prevented that and now the women reveled in the opportunity. There was lots of laughter as the women scrubbed the clothes on the wide smooth stones at river's edge, often using other stones to beat the bunched clothes to rinse and loose the ground in dirt. Narcissa pointed at the dirty and soapy water that followed the current and the ladies laughed at the bouncing bubbles. Soon they were stripped down to their undergarments and bouncing on their toes as they soaked their tired bodies in the cool water. They giggled and joked and enjoyed the refreshing time.

Unseen by anyone was the hunched figure of a man hiding in the thick willows and alders along the riverbank just upstream from the women. Thumbs stifled a cackle as he lecherously watched, squirming on his haunches. He was lost in the moment but was suddenly brought out of his leer with a clatter of hooves from behind him. He dropped behind another cluster of brush, hiding himself from the view of Marcus and Jacques, as the two men, unsuccessful in their hunt by the canyon, now trotted upstream in search of some fresh meat. When they had passed, Thumbs took one last look at the wet-headed women, now busy scrubbing one another's hair with piles of lather showing, and backed away to sneak back to the camp.

CHAPTER FOURTEEN
GROUNDWORK

TATE FOLLOWED THE PROGRESS OF SNAKE AS THE WOULD-BE bandit as he rode the trail alongside the Wind River, making his way to the Rendezvous with the other brigands. When Tate overheard the conversation of the two that had taken the Arapaho girl captive, they spoke of the plan to meet where Union Pass started up the mountain. Tate was belly down on the promontory that afforded him a panoramic view of the valley below, and he watched Snake gravitate to the huge rock pile at the edge of the trees. This was the location Tate had expected the man to choose for his camp, giving him a view of and ready access to the agreed upon meeting place. The tall pines obscured Tate's view as the man moved into the edge of the trees to make his camp, but Tate had scouted out the area and knew where Snake would be found.

With Snake tucked away in his camp below, Tate turned and scanned the lower trail where the wagons would appear. He lifted his glass to the stretch of roadway beyond the cut and as far as he could see, there was no sign of any life that didn't have four legs. He sat up, leaned against a boulder and patted the wolf pup on his head, speaking softly to him. It was the way of men in the mountains, often the only companion they had to carry on a conversation with was their horse or another animal companion. Lobo looked at his friend with wide eyed curiosity, enjoying the man's stroking of his fur. Tate looked at his friend and thought how the pup was no longer a pup. He rubbed his head and said, "Boy, you're growin' up too fast an' pretty soon you're gonna be bigger'n me. I guess that'll be alright, long's ya don't start actin' like one o' yore kinfolks and start chewin' on my leg."

"So, Lobo, we don't know for sure how many there'll be involved in this mess, aside from that Snake down below, so I'm thinkin' we need to do somethin' to put the fear into 'em. The advantage we have, is they don't know how many of us there are neither. Hmmm, whatchu think, huh? Maybe we need to take care of Snake 'fore the others get here, that'll cut down the odds a little, but we need to do sumpin' else, too." Tate looked down at the expectant face of Lobo and added, "So, you let me know if you come up with any ideas, alright?" He rolled to his knees, stood to a crouch, and moved back into the trees to make his way to his camp. He was slowly formulating a plan as he looked around at his resources.

He walked deeper into the trees, found a couple of saplings, cut them and returned to his camp to begin his preparations. He trimmed the saplings and peeled off the bark, and with considerable whittling and trimming, he shaped the saplings into the beginning of lances. Taking the deer-hide from Knuckles last kill for meat, he began cutting it into thin rawhide strips. He busied himself for a couple of hours, periodically taking a jaunt to the promontory to check for the wagons, before sitting back on the log by his fire ring and admiring his handiwork. He had used vermillion to color the lances in a bright pattern, wrapped the middle portion with rawhide as was common for a hand-grip, added some feathers for decoration and used some crudely fashioned points from an antler shed found in the woods. He was pleased with his work and thought, *Now I need something a little grisly, bloody maybe, to make it really scary.* He looked around his camp, seeing nothing, and considered what he could use. As he thought, he made another trip to the promontory to see if there were any wagons enroute. There were none.

He wasn't certain about what he was to do, without knowing how many he would be up against and what they were planning, he was at a definite disadvantage. But he knew what they did not, the planned meeting with their cohorts would not take place, their plan would have to change and when your opponent has to make unexpected changes, you have the advantage. He stood and stretched, looked at Lobo lounging near the big log, and knew he was going to have to confront Snake and remove him from the problem to improve his odds in the coming conflict. *I think I'll wait till dusk, take him when he's thinkin' about sleeping instead of fighting.* He looked at Lobo, stroked his head and said, "Yeah, boy, that's what we'll do." He lifted his eyes to the sky to determine how much time remained before dusk, placed a couple of sticks on the coals and moved the coffee pot closer.

The sun was just past the crest of the hill when Tate started down the steep slope, working his way through the thick timber. The woods were littered with dense deadfall from long past heavy winters and blowdowns, he had to watch every step with the abundance of dried branches that covered the ground. With the steep grade, deadfall, and rocky ground with slippery pine needles, he was challenged to keep his approach silent, but he moved as quietly as a hawk in flight, a skill honed by his years alone in the wilderness. He smelled the smoke of Snake's fire, heard him moving around, digging in his packs and talking to himself, disgruntled with being alone.

Tate slowly and surreptitiously approached, Hawken cradled in the crook of his arm, wanting to be within a short stone's throw from the man before announcing his presence. He worked his way from tree to tree, easily hidden behind the big ponderosa that covered the lower edge of the hillside. When he neared the clearing, seeing Snake bending over the fire, Tate stepped silently into the open and said, "What's for supper?"

Snake whirled around to face the intruder to his camp, his right hand held to his hip and left hand extended as if it could stop any approach. He snarled, "You! I thot you'd gone! Whatchu doin' here?" he asked as he dropped into a slight crouch.

"What are you doin' here? You said you were leavin' these mountains!" answered Tate.

The man slowly straightened up, still slightly sideways to Tate, keeping his right side away from Tate's view. "Oh, I'ma leavin' shore 'nuff! I hadta make camp 'n rest muh horses, thasall."

Tate relaxed and started to put a foot up on a nearby log, looked to see where he placed his foot, and in that instant Snake brought his second whip up, and in one quick crack, snatched the rifle from Tate's relaxed grip. Tate knew he was in trouble. He grabbed for his Colt, and brought it from the holster, only to have it snapped out of his hand by the cutting tip of the bullwhip. Tate dropped into a crouch, arms outstretched, and watched Snake flip the whip back and forth, taunting him. Snake snarled, "Now, I'm gonna cut you to pieces. You kilt muh partner, now I'm gonna make you bleed!" As he spoke he sidestepped, making the whip dance behind him, grinning at Tate.

The whip whistled through the air, and the fall and the

popper struck like a knife, cutting through the buckskin of Tate's tunic. Without the buckskin, his hide would have been laid open to the bone. Tate grabbed at the thong of the whip, missing as Snake brought it back quicker than the strike of a viper. He lashed out again and again, each time scoring a hit. Tate's body began to show blood from wounds to his shoulders and upper arms. Suddenly, the whip lashed at his thigh and cut into his britches, but did not bring blood. Tate moved side to side, trying to anticipate when the next strike would come. He watched the eyes of Snake, noticing that before each strike, they would flare wide in evil anticipation.

"He he he, I'm enjoyin' this! I'm gonna make you bleed, and you're gonna scream for mercy, but you ain't gittin' none!" Another strike whistled through the air and Tate successfully stepped away, making the man miss. Snake snarled, "That's O.K., I like to see you dance! It just makes it last longer, but you're still gonna bleed all over this mountain!" He struck again, missed, but the crack of the popper on the end of the whip sounded like a rifle shot that echoed back from the mountain. The two adversaries were circling one another like animals in a fight to the death. Snake was certain he was going to cut Tate to ribbons and was savoring every strike. He became confident that he would kill the man, certain that Tate did not have a chance to defend himself. He was the kind of assailant that always had to have everything in his favor, the idea of an equal contest was never considered. His kind never attacked alone, unless the odds were overwhelming in his favor, and now he was certain he would destroy this man.

As Tate carefully watched every movement of the man, he began to anticipate and avoid the last three strikes. Snake realized he was missing, and his frustration rose with his anger, more determined to kill the man before him and do it quickly. Each strike bore more vengeance and force, making the whip whistle faster and strike harder and Tate felt the last strike as the whip lashed over his shoulder and the popper tear his back. He saw his Colt lying in the dust, made a motion toward it and was seen by Snake. The attacker thought he knew what Tate was going to do and when Tate feinted to his left as if he was going to dive for the pistol, Snake brought the whip forward, hoping to tear flesh from the man. Suddenly from the side of the clearing, a growling grey streak flew through the air, fangs bared and searching for the throat of Snake. Lobo came in a terrifying attack. Snake threw up his arms in defense knocking the wolf aside. What he didn't see was Tate's sudden movement to bring his Bowie from the sheath at his back, and in one lightning fast motion made an underhand throw, burying the razor-sharp Bowie's long blade to the hilt in the chest of Snake. The whip wielder froze, looked down at the handle of the knife, and knew he was dead. He lifted his eyes to Tate with an expression of hatred and fear, looked back at the knife and fell to his face in the dust. Lobo tore at the man's dirty buckskins until Tate called him off.

Using the toe of his moccasin, Tate rolled Snake to his back, looked at the sightless eyes staring into nothing, and withdrew his knife from the man's chest. He wiped the blade on the man's tunic and stepped back away from the body. He looked around the camp, saw nothing useful, except for the man's rifle and accouterments, laid them aside and went for one of the tethered horses. He let the horse do the work as he pulled the man's body to a nearby draw, started to drop the body down, then decided to take the bloody buckskin shirt. After removing the shirt, he pushed the body over the edge, caved in the slope to cover it and returned to the camp for the gear and the other horse.

It was well after dark when Tate made his way by moonlight to the edge of the timber at the roadway that marked the beginning of Union Pass. He stood the two lances, in a crossed position, with the bloody tunic of Snake hanging between the points, in the center of the roadway. Using some of his trade vermillion, he prepared a cup full of the bright red dye and splashed it around the lances and across the roadway. There were other preparations in his plan, but they would wait until first light. He wanted the wagons to stop here and he was certain this would make even the experienced mountain men question what was meant. *Maybe, just maybe, it might even make 'em a little scared,* thought Tate as he chuckled to himself, picturing the reaction of the travelers.

CHAPTER FIFTEEN
SUSPICION

It was the beginning of the second week under the guidance of Jacques and Thumbs and the ladies were becoming more relaxed and confident in their scouts. Both men had proved capable and generous in their provision of game meat, their manners had improved somewhat, although their crude natures occasionally surfaced, and the travel had been without any exceptional challenges. The Wind River mountains lingered on the western horizon, tantalizing in their promise of cooler and greener trails. The travelers had been longing to see the mountains since they began this wagon trip just over two months ago. The sight of mountains still holding patches of snow stood in stark contrast to the dusty trails they traveled across the great plains. But it was more than the sight of snowcapped mountains, but the promise and assurance that the mountains were the last obstacle before they would reach their destination in the northern plains. The home of the Nez Perce, Cayuse and Blackfoot Indians was where they were determined to begin their ministry by providing education and Bible teaching to the natives.

After their stop when they crossed the river, having enjoyed the time to wash clothes and bathe themselves, the refreshed travelers had an early start. They were now entering the Wind River valley with its wide flats that stretched between the Wind River Mountains and the smaller Owl Creek mountains. The mouth of the valley was about fifty miles wide and held a variety of landscapes; from low rolling hills, to flat top buttes with rimrock and wide expanses of sagebrush, cactus, and buffalo grass, all framed by the mountains.

The Whitman wagon was in the lead, as the four wagons rotated, with Gray and Price following and the Spalding wagon trailing behind. Jacques rode up alongside the Whitmans and told Marcus, "We'll need to keep a sharp eye out. This hyar's Arapaho and Crow country. Sometimes e'en some Cheyenne or Sioux show up, but the Crow are from the Absaroka," he pointed to distant mountains barely seen in the north, "and the 'rapaho claim all the Wind River mountains. But bof' of 'em come down in the valley to hunt. Thar's usually buffler down hyar in the flats, sometimes elk and lots o' antelope. Ain't none of 'em too friendly and I ain't certain any of 'em ever seen a wagon train. Thar's been some wagons come this way to Ronnyvous, but them was traders an' the injuns like tradin', but wagons wit' wimmen and such, I dunno. So, keep an eye out!" he warned as he reined away, "Oh, an, me'n Thumbs'll be ridin' on ahead to check the trail and get some more game. Also, be lookin' fer Injuns so if we see them 'fore they see us, we can defend ourselves better." He waved off and kneed his horse to catch up with Thumbs.

When they stopped for the noon break, Jacques had dropped off a fresh kill of mule deer and the women gladly fried up some thin cut steaks with wild vegetables, fresh biscuits and gravy. Jacques and Thumbs joined the gathering, enthusiastic in their praise of such a lavish meal for midday and were told the evening meal would be leftovers from this repast. The men looked at one another and smiled at the women folk. William Gray spoke for them all when he said, "Ladies, even the leftovers from a meal like this is better than what most men in the mountains would have for a whole summer. Thank you." The other men echoed his praise and the women beamed with the compliments.

Marcus asked Jacques, "How long do you think it'll be before we get to this pass you spoke of?"

"Wal, all depends, but countin' today, we'll prob'ly reach thar by the end of the week, give or take," answered Jacques.

"And how long to get over the mountains?" asked Reverend Spalding.

"Oh, it'll only be a couple days, that is, if'n we don't have no trouble. Then we drop into another valley an' travel'll be 'bout like 'dis," he commented, waving his arm around to indicate the nearby terrain.

"So, we're still on schedule then?" inquired William Gray.

"Yup, yup, still on schedule," muttered Jacques, with a mouthful of steak.

When the wagons resumed their trek, Jacques and Thumbs were riding a couple of miles in front of the wagons when Thumbs protested, "I'm almighty tired o' bein' so all fired nice to them pilgrims! Makes me wanna slit thar throats ever' time they ask some fool question!"

"Now, don't go gettin' yore sef' all riled up, we'll git thar soon 'nuff. An' when we got more men, it'll make it all that much easier to git the job done," assured Jacques.

"Wal, I got muh eye on that young wench. I'ma gonna take her an' make her mine!" declared Thumbs, cackling at the thought.

"Uh, you might wanna rethink that. I recomember that one. She'd just as soon slit yore throat as look atchu."

"Whatchu mean? You knowed her?" asked a dumb-founded Thumbs.

"Ummhumm, wal, I didn't know her, just knowed about her. She used to work the line in some o' them river towns. She's older'n she looks, meaner too."

"You don't say, wal, I'll be durned. If'n that don't beat all. But she's still a looker!"

WITH ALL THE days running together and each the same as the last, the week passed quickly. Jacques called a halt of the wagons when the trail was crossing a wide expanse of green grass that came from the river bank and stretched to the hills to the east. The wide valley had closed in on them and they were now between the foothills of the Wind River mountains and the scraggly beginning of the Absaroka range. The towering spires and needles of the Absaroka were awe-inspiring for the members of the missionary group, with the deep gouged ravines and tree-lined gullies that pointed upwards to the rocky fingers that seemed to be clawing at the blue of the sky. With the Absaroka stretching across the north and the Wind River mountains showing their spine of peaks lining the south, the travelers felt miniscule and insignificant in this wild country.

As they prepared camp, they spoke in soft tones as if afraid to disturb the stillness of the wilderness. With the easy breeze whispering through the pines and across the grassy flats, they were reminded of the waves of the ocean as the foxtail grasses moved with a rhythm heard only by the nature lover. The chuckling of the waters that came from the Wind River as it cascaded away from the mountains provided a backdrop for the symphony of the shadowy mountains. At the suggestion of Jacques, the men had gone to the river to try their luck at catching some trout for a change for their evening meal. The women had two dutch ovens with fresh biscuits sitting near the fires with hot coals underneath and on top.

The women sat together, content with a few moments by themselves with no pressing duties and were enjoying the companionship. Eliza said to no one in particular, "Is it just me, or have any of you noticed that Jacques and Thumbs seem to have become a little more surly in their manner the last few days?"

No one answered right away, each appearing to be thinking about the question, when Narcissa answered, "Yes, I think so. But they've still provided the meat and haven't been quite as offensive in their manner as they were before. It's probably just that they're tired just like we are, I'm hoping we'll get to take a rest day soon."

The other ladies nodded their heads in agreement, but Amy and Melissa Price made no comment. Eliza responded, "Yes, I'd like that too. But we must make time while we can. When we saw those Indians, what was that, two days ago? I was afraid we would be attacked, I was so scared. I certainly don't want to waste any time or be caught by those Arapaho, I think that was what our scouts called them." Her nervousness was evident as she flounced around, trying to find a more comfortable seat.

"Why Eliza, if you feel that way about the natives, why are you with us? We are going to establish a mission to other Indians, and I don't see how these would be any different, do you?" asked Narcissa.

Eliza squirmed a bit and looked at her friend hoping she would answer, "Oh, I believe we should try to reach all that we can for the Lord's sake, but, I don't know, it just scares me to think that these same Indians have killed other white men, and, well, you've heard the stories too. You know, how they don't treat their captives very well."

"Well, my friend, we must trust in the Lord to take care of us. Remember His promise in Hebrews, "I will never leave thee, nor forsake thee, so that we may boldly say, The Lord is my helper, and I will not fear what man shall do unto me."

"Yes, you're right. I just can't help myself sometimes," resolved Eliza.

Narcissa looked to the river and saw the men coming to their camp, two of them carrying a sizable stringer of trout. She smiled and turned back to the ladies and said, "Well, looks like our loafing time is over. We've got a bunch of fish to fry!"

The ladies rose and began preparing things for the evening meal, anticipating the taste of the fresh trout. Jacques and Thumbs had not returned, but they knew the two scouts would not miss another opportunity for a good meal prepared by the ladies. After all, it would still be a little while before everything was ready.

CHAPTER SIXTEEN
SCOUT

Tate finished the rest of his preparation by the grey light of early morning. He climbed back to his promontory and took up his vigil, expecting to see the wagons soon. With nothing to see, he stretched out, covered his eyes with his floppy hat, and enjoyed a bit of a snooze, warmed by the bright sun of midday. By mid-afternoon he spotted the white bonnets of four wagons following the winding trail that paralleled the Wind River. He followed their progress with the aid of his telescope, sitting on his haunches and using his crossed legs to support his elbows holding his scope still. Two riders led the wagons about two miles ahead and moving at an easy gait. He saw the leader of the two drop from his mount and take a shot at a mule deer and miss. The men rode back to the wagons and stopped the group for their evening camp. The wagons were just past the cut where the valley narrowed, allowing just enough room for the trail to crawl over a finger of the hillside that protruded across the valley floor. Tate followed their example and returned to his camp for some fresh coffee and pemmican.

He thought about the forthcoming conflict, uneasy with

the not knowing what awaited. He did not know which of the men were the threat, which ones were to be the victims, and when anything was to happen. He was hoping the outriders would reveal themselves when they saw the warning lances or perhaps even sooner. As he considered the possibilities, he thought surely the perpetrators of the proposed massacre and robbery would come looking for the two men that were to meet them before the attack, and if they did, they would then be known to Tate. He knew he had to be watchful and certain of their intentions as he could not cut down on innocents. He could think of no other preparations he could make and determined to trust his judgment, believing he had planned well, at least as well as he could under the circumstances.

When he returned to the point, he resumed his position and took up his telescope to watch the activity of the wagons. The two riders were just coming over the narrow knoll when he lifted his scope. The cut was less than a mile away and he knew the men would soon be to the river crossing just below. He crabbed his way off the point and grabbed his Hawken and gear and started through the trees toward the site that had been Snake's camp. He wanted to be in place before the men arrived, so he could be close enough to hear any conversation. Within moments, he was in position behind a small cluster of boulders and saplings. He dropped to one knee, totally hidden from view of the campsite, but with a line of sight through the aspen saplings to the clearing. He waited.

The splashing of water and clatter of hooves announced the presence of the two men. As expected, they made their way to the mound of boulders, ready to find their two partners. When they rode into the clearing, Jacques said, "Now where are they? I tol' 'em to be here an' wait! Didn't I? You heerd me!"

"Yeah, I heerd you, Jacques. I don' know where they be," answered Thumbs. Jacques stepped down from his saddle, followed by Thumbs, and began looking around.

Tate had chosen to leave enough sign that these men would believe their friends had been here, but he didn't know it they were good enough to tell what had happened. He watched as Jacques dropped to one knee and put his hand to the ground, tracing the tracks of the horses. He looked carefully at the sign in the dirt, lifted his head in the direction of the ravine where Tate covered the body of Snake, and back at the tracks in the clearing. He looked at Thumbs and said, "They was here, but I think Injuns might'a got 'em. Ain't nuthin' but moccasin tracks an the hosses 'er gone." He stood and looked at the edge of the clearing where another mound of rocks marked the tree line. He walked to the rocks and looked behind the pile to see some of the gear that belonged to Snake, scattered about. "See hyar! Some o' thar' gear, stuff the Injuns wouldn't want, just some junk. Yup, Injuns got 'em," he declared as he walked back to his mount and stepped into the stirrup to swing aboard. When Thumbs was seated, he looked to Jacques and asked, "Now whadda we do?" as he looked nervously around, expecting to see Indians ready to attack.

Jacques leaned his arms on the saddle horn and looked to his partner and said, "We do just as we planned, we'll take 'em when we git hyar. Onliest thing is, we gotta do it differnt. Come'eer," he instructed as he reined his horse around to return to the roadway. As they rode from the clearing, Tate followed, staying well covered by the thick timber, trotting through the trees to the roadway. He wanted to see their reaction when they saw the lances.

As they came to the roadway, Jacques led the way and started up the slight incline, keeping his eyes on the nearby trees. As they neared the lances, both men began thoroughly searching the trees, then turned back to the roadway when the horses stopped of their own accord. There, immediately before them, were the crossed lances with the red splashed about on the rocks of the trail. When the men spotted the sign, their heads swiveled side to side, searching for any sign of Indians. Seeing none, they dropped back into their saddles and looked at the warning. Seeing the tunic, split, cut and bloody, Thumbs said, "Uh, ain't that Snake's shirt? See the fringe at the pocket, he cut that to do up that bandage, remember? An' look at the blood! They done kilt him!" When he said 'kilt' he stood in his stirrups and nervously searched the tree line again. "Let's git outta hyar!" he pleaded as he started to rein his horse around.

"Wait a minit!" commanded Jacques. "There ain't no Injuns hyar now, if they was, we'd done been kilt our ownselves! Now, this has giv'n me a idear. Here's what we're gonna do. When we bring the wagons up in the mornin', you'n me'll hang back by the river 'n let them pilgrims find this," he motioned to the lances. "Then we'll act like we ain't never seen it, but we'll use it as an excuse to make 'em circle up down thar," he stood in his stirrups and motioned to the flat beside the road and the river. "Then when no attack comes, you'n me'll take to the trees like we're lookin' fer Injuns an' we'll take cover, make out like we been attacked, an' then we can shoot the pilgrims from the trees, just like we was Injuns!"

"Won't they be shootin' back?" whined Thumbs.

"Course they will, but ain't none of 'em can hit nuthin', cep'in maybe Price, but we don't have to worry 'bout him. All told, thar's only four men and four wimmen, shouldn't take long to git it done. Then we can take their little treasure chest and head to Californy!"

"But don't shoot that young one, I tol you I want her!"

"Humph, we'll see 'bout that tomorrow," declared Jacques as he reined his mount around to start back to the wagons.

Tate waited until they crossed the finger knoll at the cut in the valley, then rose to arrange his previous preparations to give him the advantage during the coming 'Indian attack' planned by the two scouts. He shook his head as he thought of the evil on men's minds and how they could justify any action when motivated by nothing but greed. He remembered his Pa talking about the book of Proverbs saying those that were *greedy of gain . . . taketh away the life of the owners.* He spoke to Lobo, "Maybe we can change that tomorrow." With his teeth showing, Lobo agreed.

CHAPTER SEVENTEEN
ATTACK

As Tate walked back to his camp, he was uneasy. He thought he had made the right plans, set things about to be ready for the feigned attack from the two renegades. But as he walked, he thought about coming events, and he became uncomfortable, knowing there were many unknowns and possibilities of everything going wrong. The missionaries would be in jeopardy during the attack and Tate would not be in control. As he thought, he realized his mistake was to depend on the action of the renegades and having to react instead of act. But it would be to his greater advantage to take the battle to them instead of waiting for their action. He knew who his opponents were, now it would be up to him to turn the tables on them and take the initiative. All he had accomplished with the warning lances was to allow them to adjust their plan to their benefit. Putting them on the defensive would give Tate a greater advantage. He sat down and begin to reassess the plan and formulate a new one.

The black veil of night was slowly lifting as the early light began pushing its way above the eastern horizon. Low lying clouds were soon painted a brilliant red, reminding Tate of the old sailor's mantra, *Red sky at night, sailor's delight. Red sky at morning, sailor's take warning.* He grinned to himself and thought, *Renegades take warning!*

He was well hidden on the far side of the river, yet atop a slight knoll that gave him a view of the camp of the wagons and the road way that would take them to the pass. First light saw activity in the camp, women at the early morning fires for their coffee and first meal, while the men gathered the mules and harnessed the animals. Soon, most were finishing their meal and returning to the final preparations for the day's journey when Tate saw the two guides mounting up to start their planned scout well ahead of the wagons.

There was a single stubborn cedar that tenaciously clung to the rockpile with roots that dug into narrow cracks, grasping at what little soil had been blown there by long ago winds. With the rockpile surrounded on three sides by the black timber, the mound protruded into the valley like the belly of a town drunk yet afforded Tate with an excellent bastion to launch his attack. The single cedar gave just enough camouflage and cover to conceal his position. He watched as the two riders started up the slight grade that would take them over the finger knoll and around the point. He readied himself as they crested the knoll and suddenly drew up. They were stopped by the crossed lances in the roadway, that stood below the crest of the hill, just out of sight of the camp.

When they stopped, they looked around nervously and Tate let fly his first arrow. The missile whispered its way to the ground right in front of the warning lances. Jacques screamed as he jumped from the saddle, taking cover behind his horse and looking over the seat of the saddle, searching for the band of Indians he was certain were attacking.

Thumbs also stood behind his horse, but he was searching for some other cover that would afford greater safety. "Can you see 'em?" asked Thumbs.

"No! I cain't see nuthin'!" declared Jacques. He had slipped his rifle from the scabbard and had it laying across the saddle as he searched for a target.

Thumbs remembered Jacques screaming and said, "You screamed like a woman! I thought you was snake bit or sumpin'."

"I didn't scream!" snarled Jacques.

"You did too! An' you weren't even hit! I ain't never heard a grown man scream," responded Thumbs, laughing.

Suddenly another arrow found its mark in the pommel of the saddle, inches from Jacques' rifle, and he screamed again. Thumbs jumped when both horses spooked, and the men fought to keep them still. The animals were their only cover and nothing else was near enough to get to without taking an arrow.

Jacques fired his rifle, taking a random shot toward the willows by the river. He knew the usual range for a bow and thought the Indians had to be under the cover of the riverside brush and trees. His horse had grown nervous from the behavior of his rider, and the rifle shot made him jerk free, kicking back at Jacques as the man fought to get the reins. But the frightened animal moved too fast for the man and the resulting commotion caused Thumbs horse to join in the fray. Within seconds, the men found themselves without cover and went to their bellies and began crawling toward a cluster of sage just below the trail.

Tate watched with amusement as the two scouts scrambled for the brush. He knew if the men were thinking of an Indian attack, they would believe themselves to be greatly outnumbered. He waited for them to get to cover as he watched the horses running up the trail and out of reach of the two men. With only one shot fired, he reasoned the people at the wagons would not be alarmed, thinking their scouts had taken some game for meat. He also knew they would not break camp until the scouts returned. He dropped down the back side of the boulders and trotted to his secondary position downstream a short distance, where he still had a clear line of sight. He wanted to separate the renegades from the wagons, maybe even cause them to flee the area. He was not anxious to kill again, but he was prepared for whatever may come. When he gained his second position, he sent another arrow into their cover, bringing a yelp from one of the two renegades.

"They got me!" shouted Jacques, looking at the arrow protruding from his thigh. Blood was welling around the shaft, the tip going completely through.

"I'm gonna die! I'm gonna die!" he screamed as he dropped his rifle and grabbed his thigh by the shaft of the arrow. Blood was pumping from the wound and his buckskins were already soaking it up, the excess dripping to the ground.

Thumbs undid his neckerchief and handed it to Jacques, "Here, tie this aroun' yore leg!"

Jacques looked wide-eyed at his partner and said, "You do it!"

Thumbs gave the man an exasperated look, lay his rifle aside, and reached down to wrap the leg with the neckerchief as best as it would allow, and tied it off as tight as he could. It did not appear to make any difference in the bleeding.

"Oh lordy, I'm gonna bleed ta' death!" moaned Jacques.

This was the man that had blustered his way around everyone, giving the appearance of bravery and boldness, but now when he was facing the grim reaper, he had turned to a whining and fearful coward. Such is the case with many a man that faces the reality of death knowing he has made no provisions to prepare for his eternity.

Thumbs looked around as best he could without showing himself from the scant cover. He saw nothing but knew that Indians were able to hide in plain sight and they could be anywhere. He also thought he would not have any chance of survival, one man against an entire band of Indian warriors that were obviously out to kill them. As he looked about, he saw the two horses had stopped and were grazing alongside the trail about forty yards away. He looked around, debating his chances of making it to the horses, lined out other places of cover he might make before he made it to the horses, and considered all of his chances.

"What're we gonna do?" whined Jacques. Always the man in charge, he now sought direction from his partner. He looked wide-eyed at Thumbs, waiting for an answer.

Thumbs said, "Can you run wit' that leg?" as he nodded toward the wound.

"NO! I cain't move at all!"

"If I get the horses, can you ride?"

"I cain't even move, I said. If'n I move, I'll bleed ta' death!" he argued.

"If you don't move, you're gonna be bleedin' from yore head when they scalp you!"

Jacques' hand flew to his head, realized he had lost his hat and feeling the hair on his head. He realized what Thumbs had said and he looked to his partner, fear in his eyes. "No! No! you can't let 'em scalp me!"

Thumbs looked at Jacques and knew the man had been paralyzed by his fear and would be useless in trying to make an escape. He looked at the man again, turned to look at the horses, and realized he would have to make his own escape or stay with Jacques and be killed by the Indians. The two men had ridden together for three years, worked together to pull off some robberies and killings, but their friendship was one of convenience not commitment. He knew if the tables were turned, Jacques would not hesitate to leave him behind if it meant he might escape. That thought helped Thumbs to make up his mind.

"Look, we cain't stay here, them Injuns'll be on us real soon. Th' onliest way we can git outta here is fer me to get them horses." He picked up Jacques' rifle and said, "I'm gonna load your rifle. Now, you'll take a shot when I say, an' I'll take off after the horses. You'll need to reload and be ready to shoot when I start back with 'em, ya' hear?"

Jacques looked at his friend, down at his rifle, watched as Thumbs loaded the weapon, and mumbled a "Yeah, I hear."

Tate had also seen the horses stop to graze and he decided to move up the valley to give himself a better view of the horses and the roadway between the two renegades and the animals. He had no sooner taken his position at the tree line, when a shot from the cluster of sage that had been the men's cover caught his attention. He looked to the brush, saw Thumbs rise and start to run toward the horses, and Tate fired another arrow at the running man. He did not aim to kill, just to frighten, and the arrow hit the ground just a pace ahead of Thumbs, making him stumble and fall headlong into the dirt.

Thumbs scrambled to all fours, so afraid he didn't realize he dropped his rifle. He made like a scared rabbit as he sought protection behind another cluster of sage. When he was behind the brush, he dropped to his belly, shaking.

Tate chuckled at the antics of the man, knowing if the two outlaws were to realize one man was responsible for this big Indian attack, they would probably die from embarrassment. But he wasn't about to let them know who was responsible for their dilemma. He looked at the horses, brought his Hawken from his back where it hung on its sling, and placed a cap on the nipple. He lifted the rifle to his shoulder, cocked the hammer and set the triggers, lined up the front blade sight with the buckhorns at the rear and squeezed off a shot. The slug hit the hard-packed trail just behind the horses and sent them running again. Tate knew this time they would be well out of reach of Thumbs.

He heard Jacques call out to his partner, "Are you hit?"

"No, but it was close. The horses spooked again an' I cain't get to 'em!" shouted Thumbs to his partner.

"Can you make it back here?" pleaded Jacques.

"Not alive, I cain't. Why?"

"Cuz I'ma bleedin' an I cain't stop it!" whined Jacques.

"Well, I cain't do nuthin' 'bout it," answered Thumbs.

Tate chuckled at the talk of the men, considering what he might do with them. He stood his Hawken against the tree, picked up his bow and nocked an arrow. He sent the shaft into the cover of the sage that protected Thumbs and heard the man shout in alarm. Tate, still well concealed, shouted to Thumbs, "You! White man! Take horse, go! No come back!" He tried his best to sound like an angry Indian and watched as Thumbs slowly lifted his head to look in his direction.

"How do I know you won't shoot when I go get muh horse?" cried Thumbs.

"Go! Now! Stay, die!" answered Tate in a gravelly voice.

Thumbs wasn't concerned about his partner and suddenly stood and took off at a run toward the horses, both had again stopped to enjoy the green grass at river's edge. Tate watched as Thumbs staggered to his horse, spoke to the animal and holding his arms wide, successfully caught up the reins. With a quick glance over his shoulder, he mounted up and dug his heels into the ribs of his horse and leaning well over its neck, he put it to a gallop and made for the roadway and the Union Pass. Tate watched with a sense of relief, thinking now there was just one to deal with, and turned to look toward the first cluster of sage for any sign of life. He waited for almost a half hour before he started from his cover toward the sage.

Holding his Hawken before him, he stealthily walked to the brush, saw no movement and shook the sagebrush with the muzzle of the Hawken. Nothing. He spoke, "Don't move or you'll get a bullet!" There was no response. He carefully walked around the brush, saw the extended legs of Jacques, and as the rest of the man came into view, he saw a white faced, open eyed corpse. The man had bled out from the wound in his thigh that cut his femoral artery. Tate looked at the man, let out a heavy sigh, withdrew the arrow and turned away to fetch his other arrows and return to his camp. He would check the trail of Thumbs to make sure he was well on his way away from the area, then he would gather his gear and go to the camp of the wagons and give them the story of their renegade scouts. But first, he'd have to see to Lobo and maybe have some coffee and a bit of grub.

CHAPTER EIGHTEEN
BETRAYAL

Tate led the remuda toward the wagons. He rode Shady, led two pack horses and a spare, two horses from Snake, and Jacques' horse with his body tied over the saddle. It was quite a sight for the missionaries as they gathered to watch the buckskin attired man of the mountains ride into their camp with a wolf laying across the rump of his horse. He was almost to the group when Nathan Price called out to the others, "Hey, he's got Jacques tied on this one!"

The startled group looked beyond Tate to see Nathan lifting the head of their scout and looking to the group. Marcus Whitman looked at the young man and said, "What's the meaning of this? Why do you have our scout? What happened to him, and where's Thumbs?"

Tate sat silent, waiting for the man to at least pause to give him an opportunity to answer. Their stern expressions told of doubt and suspicion of this stranger that came unbidden into their camp. He noticed the speaker motion to another man and watched as that man retrieved a rifle from a wagon. Another man, bearded and attired in all black with a flat crowned black hat, stepped forward and said, "I am the

Reverend Henry Spalding and I am the leader of this group. The body that you have tied on that horse yonder is our scout and guide, Jacques LaRamee." Tate showed surprise at the name, but let the speaker continue. The reverend added, "Now, we expect an explanation."

Tate looked from one to another, and not receiving an invitation to step down, he lay the reins of Shady across his pommel, hooked his leg over the horn, patted the head of Lobo and leaned on his knee, "Well, it's kind of a long story, so, feel free to pull up a seat."

"Young man, we want an explanation and we want it right now!" demanded the reverend.

Tate smiled and said, "Has anybody here been prayin' for the Lord to send some help?"

His reference to prayer and the Lord surprised the entire group, and they looked at one another until Narcissa quietly spoke up, "Yes, I have felt for some time that we needed some help and I have been asking the Lord to give us His protection."

The reverend looked at the woman and said, "Well, Narcissa, we've all been praying for God's guidance for this entire trip. Why would your prayer be any different?"

"Because I have been quite unsettled about the two scouts and believed we were not safe in their hands," she explained. When she spoke, Eliza stepped next to her friend and added, "Nor have I, and yes, I have joined my sister in prayer for God's guidance about those men."

The reverend looked from Narcissa to his wife, back to Narcissa, and then to Tate and asked, "And just what concern is that of yours, young man?"

"Well, you see reverend, for some time now I've had this tuggin' at my soul urging me down thisaway, and I couldn't tell just what it was, until . . . " and he began to explain about his first encounter with Snake and his partner and the Indian girl they had taken captive. "And while I listened, they talked about their plans to meet up with a couple of fellas named Jacques and Thumbs, and what they spoke about wasn't too pleasant. When I confronted them, things didn't go so well for one of 'em, but the other'n, wal, I give him a chance to get clear of this country and forget about his plans. But, . . . " and Tate continued to tell them about the plan of the men to take the missionaries money and skedaddle to California, but he omitted the bloodier portions of the story. When the reverend said, "But, we would not have surrendered that money, they wouldn't be able to just take it and leave."

"They didn't plan on any of you being able to object," stated Tate, letting his words lay heavy on their minds before they understood. Narcissa put her hand to her mouth as she took a startled breath, and asked, "You mean . . .?"

"Yes ma'am, that's exactly what they meant to do. But when I met up with them this mornin', well, as you can see," nodding his head toward the last horse in the line, "Jacques kinda changed his mind. Oh, and by the way, I don't know what his real name was, but the real Jacques LaRamee died several years back. He was an old-timer in these mountains. Now, Thumbs, when I suggested he make tracks, he up jumped and ran lickety split! 'pears he was a bit smarter than his partner."

"Now, just why should we believe you, a complete stranger?" asked a rather exasperated Marcus. "Who's to say you didn't just kill both of our scouts and plan to try to rob us yourself?"

Tate looked at the man with a bland expression and quietly responded, "Sir, whatever your name is, you're not back east in the city and you best not conduct yourself as if you were. What you just said, with anyone else, could get you killed real easy. You accused me of murder and of planning to rob you, now there's a lot of men in this country that would take affront to such an accusation. But just this once, I will overlook your ignorance. I will leave you with your scout and his horse and be on my way." He slowly brought his leg across the pommel, put his foot in the stirrup and reined his horse around to leave. The group stood still, shocked at what they had heard and seen, but no one made a move to stop the young man. With pack horses in tow, he started toward the horse with the body, reached down to untie the lead rope, tossed it over the neck of the horse and started to leave.

He had not looked back at the group, but the sudden call from the reverend said, "Wait, please." Tate turned in the saddle to look back toward the group and watched as the reverend walked toward him. The older man looked up and asked, "Young man, I apologize for our rudeness. You have come to help and we have offered nothing but suspicion and doubt. Will you please step down and abide with us a while, perhaps share a meal with us?"

Tate looked at the reverend, back to the crowd, all of whom stood with expectant faces, and said, "I'd be pleased to Reverend."

As he stepped down, the man asked, "May I ask your name, young man?"

"Yessir, my name's Tate Saint."

The missionary did a double take as he looked at this young man of the mountains and asked, "Did you say your name is Saint?"

"Yessir, Tate Saint."

"Well, my, my, my, will wonders never cease. Please, join us by my wagon."

The group had broken up and turned to their duties. The fire had been kindled and Narcissa and Eliza were busy preparing the evening meal with biscuits in the dutch ovens, a variety of wild vegetables in a pot hanging from a tripod, and meat frying in a pair of skillets at fire's edge. Marcus picked up the coffee pot and began filling cups, offering the first to Tate with, "I do apologize for my brash remark. I was surprised and well, . . ." Tate waved away his explanation and nodded his head as he accepted the coffee. Lobo found an inconspicuous place to lie beside his master.

Tate looked around at those that were gathered, saw three men and two women, looked beyond the circle and saw no one else nearby and turned back to the fire. He remembered Jacques and Thumbs saying there were four men and four women, and at that thought he turned to Reverend Spalding and asked, "Is there someone missing? When I overheard the two planning their deed, they said there were only four men and four women, but I don't see that many here."

The missionary smiled and said, "Oh yes, there is another family, the Prices. Nathan and his wife, Amy, and daughter Melissa. They often keep to themselves, but sometimes join us. Their wagon is that one over there," as he pointed to the last wagon in the circle. As Tate looked, he saw the glow of a campfire beyond the wagon and figured the family was there. He lifted his eyes to the sky, calculated there was about two hours of daylight left, and nodded to the missionary understanding his explanation. He thought, *So, the daughter is the one Jacques spoke of that wasn't who they thought. Interesting.*

His attention turned to Marcus as the man looked to the Reverend and spoke what the others had already been thinking as he said, "So, brother Spalding, what do we do now? No scouts or guides, in the middle of Indian country, not sure how to get where we need to go . . ."

"Yes, Marcus, I know. But perhaps the Lord has already seen our dilemma and is at work on our behalf." He looked at Tate and asked, "So, Tate, do you know this country?" as he waved his arm toward the mountains.

"Well, I know a little about this country, but I'm not a

scout or a guide. This is my first time in these mountains, but I have seen some of it and know about some. Just where are you folks headed?"

"We are bound to Oregon country, specifically the land of the Nez Perce, Cayuse and Blackfeet. We are going to start mission work to provide education and Bible teaching to the native people."

Tate looked at the man, then to the others, and waited a bit as he thought about what they were doing and planned to do, he let a slow grin paint his face as he looked up. He asked, "Have any of you been to this country before, or worked with those people before?"

His question showed no skepticism or doubt, just curiosity and the reverend noted the tone of the question before he replied, "Our brother here, Marcus Whitman, has been with those very people and promised to return with more helpers to work with them. We," motioning to the others, "have all committed ourselves to this mission."

"Interesting. Well, you certainly have your work cut out for you. Now, I haven't heard anything but good about the Nez Perce, nothing about the Cayuse, but, I've heard plenty about the Blackfeet, and ain't none of it good!"

"Have you had any dealings with Indians, Tate?" asked Narcissa.

He looked at the curious woman and answered, "Yes'm, I have. I've lived around or dealt with or fought, the Osage, the Kiowa, Comanche, Apache, Ute and most recently the Shoshone and Arapaho. So, yes, I'm acquainted with the native people of this country."

She looked up from her work, surprised at his response, and said, "And what do you think of the native people?"

"Most of 'em are fine folks. Not much different than you and me. But most of 'em have their own ideas about the creator and the hereafter. Some of those beliefs are not too different than ours, and a lot of those people are quite willing to learn more about the Lord Jesus. However, there are also some of their shamans or medicine men that feel threatened by any white man that speaks of anything different than what they believe."

"And, what about you, do you know the Lord Jesus as Savior?" asked Narcissa.

"Yes'm, I accepted Christ at my mother's knee when I was a youngster. My father saw to my education, what with him being a teacher, and kept that teaching in line with the Scriptures."

The conversation of the group was interrupted suddenly by the appearance of Nathan Price and Amy as they approached, both holding rifles pointed toward the group. Tate was the first to see them and immediately stood to his feet, Lobo beside him, growling, and faced them. He was stopped at the loud command from Nathan, "Don't move! Don't none of you move! I'll shoot if I have to!" he warned as he came closer, Amy following close behind.

Tate dropped a hand to the head of Lobo and spoke softly, "Easy boy, easy."

The man's countenance was one of anger and determination as he explained, "We're leaving!" and looked at Tate as he said, "We're takin' three of your horses and leaving. Don't none of you try to follow, and you," looking directly at Tate, "don't you follow either. If any one of you tries to come after us, I'll kill the girl!"

Narcissa and Eliza gasped at the thought and Narcissa said, "But she's your daughter!"

"She ain't my daughter, and she," nodding to Amy, "ain't my wife! We were in this with Jacques and Thumbs, but he fixed that!" motioning to Tate. "Now, we're takin' the money and don't any of you try to follow. That girl was just extra baggage and I won't hesitate to shoot her!"

Tate stood with arms out to his sides, not wanting to spook the man into shooting, knowing any shot could hit someone with the group gathered so close together. He spoke calmly and said, "Take the horses, and welcome. But I'd advise you not to try the grulla, he's a one-man horse and he'll dump anyone that tries to ride him. But, have at the others, and welcome."

Nathan looked around, and began backing away, keeping the rifle pointed at the group. He ordered, "All o' you, sit down and turn around. Don't none o'ya move till we're gone, understand? It's only cuz y'all are missionaries that I ain't shootin' you, but if you foller me, all bets are off!"

The group sat down with their backs to the two rifles and waited. Within moments, they heard the thunder of retreating hooves and turned to see the three ride away into the twilight, taking the road leading to Union Pass. The group slowly stood, looked at the dust cloud left behind, turned to one another and Eliza spoke what the rest thought, "Well, if that don't beat all!"

CHAPTER NINETEEN
CHASE

ALTHOUGH SHE LOOKED MUCH YOUNGER, MELISSA WAS IN HER mid-twenties and had been in and out of mining camps, boom-towns, and worked the line in some of the larger cities from St. Louis west. Although she could play the part of a sweet innocent, when things turned sour, the hardened vixen showed. She led the trio as they took to the road in the twilight of the day, slapping leather and using her favorite quirt to get all the speed from her mount. At a full run, the horses were stretched out and riders were laying along their necks with manes whipping in their faces as they fled the wagons and any possible pursuit. The river crossing showed with the last light of day, bouncing from the surface of the shallow river, as the clear water of snowmelt and spring fed streams trickled over the gravelly bottom. Melissa never hesitated with her horse and they hit the water, splashing through with each hoof crashing into the shallows, sending spray flying that kicked back into the woman's face, but she never slowed. The other two followed without slowing and as the trio started up the incline of the pass. They disappeared into the black timber, but the hooves of the horses clattered on the rocky trail and Nathan called out, "We gotta stop! We'll kill these horses!"

Melissa seemed to come from her trance as she lifted her head and slowed her horse. She brought the animal to a stop, looking around at the trees, searching for some place that would provide cover and shelter. Seeing nothing, she started her mount at a walk, giving the animal his head and continuing up the trail in the quickening darkness. The big bay hung his head, breathing heavy, tongue lolling, and the girl knew they had to stop. She reined the horse off the trail and into a slight clearing near a trickling spring fed stream. It wasn't the most suitable campsite, but it would have to do, as she motioned the others to join her.

"It's about time," declared Nathan and he slipped from his saddle.

"Oh, shut up! This will suit us just fine, there's water and a little graze for the horses and you can stretch out your blankets there in those aspen." She looked at the other woman and motioned for her to join Nathan as she stripped her bedroll from behind her saddle. Amy simply nodded in agreement, and found a leaf covered patch suitable for her bedroll and was soon stretched out, finally relaxed enough to get some rest. The horses were picketed together and after drinking their fill from the small stream, were now snatching bits of grass, their grazing sounds somehow comforting to the fleeing trio.

"Now what do we do?" asked Narcissa of the reverend Spalding. The others looked to their leader as he lifted his face to their inquiry. The campfire gave light to their faces as Tate looked around the circle. There was a calmness to the group, unexpected from people who had just been robbed and threatened, and the question made Tate wonder just what these folks would want to do, here in the wilderness without any certainty of their location or immediate destination. Their leader looked to each one, then let his gaze linger on the newest addition to their midst, as he asked, "What do you think, Mr. Saint?" It was the first time the rest of the group had heard Tate referred to by that name and they looked to the young man and back to their leader with Eliza asking, "Your name is Saint?"

Tate dropped his head with a grin slowly stretching the corners of his mouth as he picked up a small stick to poke at the coals at the edge of the fire. He looked to the woman and replied, "Yes ma'am, my name is Tate Saint," then continued as he looked to Spalding, "as far as what to do, that's entirely up to you folks. I take it that those three took your money?"

"Yes, we had entrusted Amy with the keeping of our money box and keeping track of the funds," answered the leader of the group.

"And, just how much money did they take?" asked Tate.

"Well, it's not the amount that matters, but there was about $2,500."

"Will you be able to do the work, the mission work that is, without that money?"

"Perhaps, but not as quickly nor as efficiently. That money would buy supplies to last us for the first couple of years, and help us with the needs of the people," explained the reverend.

Marcus interjected, "We need that money! It goes without saying, we cannot get the supplies we will need to survive without it! But, is there anyway we can catch them?" he asked, directing the question to Tate.

"Hmmm, the way they went, there's just a couple of ways they could go, and it'll be easy enough tracking them anyway. I'm thinkin' they'll head over Union Pass an' maybe try to get supplied at the rendezvous, if it's still goin' that is."

"That would be great," enthusiastically declared Henry Spalding, "we were traveling with Sublette and Fitzpatrick before we chose to take this shorter route as suggested by Jacques. If we could make it to the rendezvous, we could resupply with Sublette and perhaps secure the services of another guide, hopefully one more dependable."

His declaration elicited several positive responses from the group until Marcus added, "But we still need to get our money back from Price! Is there a chance we can catch them, Tate?"

Tate looked around the group and focused on Marcus, "I probably could catch up to them, but there's no way you can with these wagons. But, from what I've seen of the roadway, I think it was opened by another supply train to a rendezvous at the same place, I believe you could make pretty good time." He leaned forward and looked from Whitman to Spalding to Gray and began to explain his thinking about pursuing the thieves. When he finished, he leaned back to let the men consider what he said, watching their reactions and discussion.

Finally, Spalding turned to Tate and said, "We would greatly appreciate your help in this matter, young man, but we don't want to put you in any danger."

Tate chuckled and responded, "Mr. Spalding, or Reverend, just being in this country puts one in danger. And trust me, I won't be taking any chances that would put me in added danger. Now, if this is what we're gonna do, you folks need to turn in because the next few days are going to be long and hard, probably more so than you've experienced this far." He added, "I expect you to be on the trail before first light."

PRICE AWOKE when he felt the hard toe of Melissa's boot

kicking at his side. He growled, "What?" as he rolled to his back to sit up. He looked to the treetops to see just a glimmer of morning light and back to the woman standing, hands on hips, beside the stirring form of Amy. "You can either get up and come along, or I'll leave you here with each other and you can wait for them missionaries to find you!"

Both rolled from their blankets, grumbling, and Amy asked, "Can't we at least take time for some coffee?"

"No, we've got to put some miles behind us, 'sides, you got a coffee pot an' some coffee you're hidin' somewhere? Cuz, I sure don't. Somebody was so scared an' in such a hurry to leave, we didn't bring many supplies with us!" She frowned at Nathan as she jabbed the last remark into his consciousness. "Plus, I don't doubt but that mountain man will be on our trail come first light. He don't look like much, but he managed to do in all four of those others that were supposed to do all the dirty work for us, so he's not somebody I reckon to deal with."

"I though he said Thumbs got away?" asked Amy.

"Yeah, he did, but that doesn't help us, we don't know where he went or if he's even still in this part of the country. So, don't go thinkin' that worthless coward's gonna be any help." Melissa went to the horses and led them into the bigger clearing, ground tied her own and started saddling the animal. Mumbling to herself but loud enough for the others to hear, "We shoulda taken one o' that man's pack animals, maybe it'd have some supplies." Melissa was the leader and planner of the entire escapade. When she met Jacques in the bar in Liberty, she told him about the missionaries, having overheard the conversation of some of the muleskinners with Sublette. She heard about the money the mission board had raised and given to the missionaries when she was shopping in the general store and heard the two men discussing what supplies they would need and how much that would leave of their funds. Her ears always perked up whenever money was mentioned and when she heard these men talking, she immediately began thinking about ways to relieve them of their burden. Her first step was to recruit a phony family and she easily found willing partners among her associates at the bar and entertainment business. When she included Jacques in her plan, she was certain they would soon be richer and on their way to San Francisco. But things had gone wrong, but she wasn't too displeased, because now there were fewer conspirators to share the money with and she was beginning to calculate how even that number could be dwindled.

She had often talked with Jacques and Thumbs on the sly, always picking their brains as to their location, the planned route, possible obstacles and more. Now that they were following the Union Pass route, she knew they were just a couple of days away from the location of the Rendezvous where they would find Sublette and Fitzpatrick and ample supplies for the rest of their escape. She would need a good cover story as to why they were no longer with the missionaries, but that would not be hard for someone of her imagination. She smiled to herself as she mounted up and reined around, ready to take to the trail. She was frustrated at the slowness of her partners but thought she would have to tolerate them a little longer, at least until they made the rendezvous, for Jacques had told her of the dangers of meeting up with Indians, and a woman alone would have no chance to defend herself.

AT THE SAME time the trio resumed their flight, Tate had been on their trail for almost an hour and knew he would easily catch them, maybe even before dark fell. But, he was not overly anxious to confront them until he knew more about their plans. He knew when someone was focused on plans or preparations for some other deed, their attention would not be on their pursuit, giving him a slight advantage. And with three of them, even though two were women, they could be very dangerous, and he wasn't taking any unnecessary chances, no matter how much money they had stolen.

CHAPTER TWENTY
PURSUIT

TATE HAD CHOSEN TO TIE OFF THE OTHER HORSES TO THE wagons, taking only one pack horse and the essentials with him. His grulla was well acclimated to the mountains and the black gelding had proven to be the better of the pack horses. He wanted to make good time, believing the trio of thieves would follow the roadway. He wanted to choose his own path, and with two mountain wise horses, he would not be held to the easier and longer roadway. When Tate and Knuckles visited at length before parting, the old-timer had talked about the rendezvous. Tate got the impression the man was somewhat wistful in that he would not be going to the reunion with old friends, but he encouraged Tate to go and get acquainted with the wily old mountain men that had an abundance of tales and knowledge to share with a likely apprentice. He had detailed the route of Union Pass and the location of the rendezvous and that information was what gave Tate confidence in his choice of routes. He was hopeful of getting to the rendezvous before the trio and knew he would have to make time to the limit of his horses' abilities.

The beginning of the pass made several switchbacks as it climbed into the higher mountains. Tate's previous promontory had also served him well when he surveyed the trail of the pass that moved off to the southwest behind the knoll that held his camp. By full daylight, he crested the climb and the wide plateau top and valley opened before him. He rode to the top of a slight juniper covered knoll to get a better view of the summit of the pass, about five miles distant. He stepped from his saddle, spyglass in hand and took a seat on a rock outcropping using his knees to rest his elbows and scanned the trail that led to the south and west. He picked up a slight dust cloud that he was certain was that of the trio, then he searched for an alternate route that would obscure him from their view. Keeping the towering snow-capped peak to his left, he saw where he could stay near or in the trees and be below the trail, with most of the way providing ample cover.

His choice proved to be advantageous and by nightfall, he was certain he had passed the trio and was ahead of them on the trail. From the summit of the pass, the roadway bore to the west staying in the flat country, while his chosen trail bore almost directly south, taking him over rolling hills, bluffs and around a couple of flat-top mesas and through thicker timber. But the game trails were plentiful, and the route was easy for his horses, although any attempt at taking a wagon would be disastrous. He thought of the missionaries and hoped they were staying true to their agreed upon plan to push the wagons as far and as fast as the animals would allow. They would have to follow the same roadway taken by the thieves, but that could not be helped, he just hoped they would not falter in their determination.

He stopped in the trees at the top of a long timbered ridge that overlooked a big bend of a valley below that cradled a winding river. He knew this was the Green River and the two mountains in the distance on the opposite side were exactly as Knuckles had described. He remembered the old-timer saying, "Yessir, that thar Green River wraps around them mountains like the apron strings of your mammy wrapped around her middle. Ain't no mistakin' it when you sees it, no ssir. An' you jist foller that Green down into the big valley an' that's whar the Rendezvous will be. Just tell them cussed drunks I sentcha, an' you'll be accepted jist like you was allus one of 'em. Oh, an' tell ol' Sublette, he still owes me fer them last plews, I ain't never collected ever thin' he owes, but I will, yessir."

Tate knew it would be a long day's travel before he made the valley, but he thought he might divide it up and cover some more ground tonight. He looked at the sky, stars were already strutting their stuff and there didn't appear to be any clouds. The moon, though waning into the last quarter, would provide just enough extra light that he was certain he could put a few more miles behind him. But first, both he and his horses needed a bit of a rest and some food.

IT SEEMED he couldn't swivel his head fast enough to take in all the sights around him. With pack horse trailing behind, he negotiated his way through the maze of tipis, wall tents, brush huts, and other contraptions that served as shelters for the conglomeration of men and Indians. He noted different encampments that appeared to be separate villages of Indians, and each one seemed to be of different tribes, but the Indians and mountain men mixed as if there were no boundaries or differences. As he rode into the gathering, most of those nearby would give him a once over, but not recognizing the man would return to their doings, paying no heed to the newcomer.

There appeared to be a cluster of structures on a higher point of the valley that gave the appearance as the center of the activity. Tate assumed these would be the shelters of the traders and pointed the grulla toward the tents and lean-tos. With no one paying him any particular attention, he stepped down from his mount, tied them off to the hitch rail, and walked up to the wide plank counters that were mounded with peltries and other goods. Three men behind the counters were busy with their bickering customers as they argued back and forth over the quality mouand prices for the pelts. Tate stepped to the side to wait his turn and was soon greeted with, "Howdy there younker, what can we do you fer?"

Tate saw the man was leaning against the counter to support himself and noted a crutch leaning against an upright nearby. The missionaries had described Sublette as a man with one wooden leg and using a crutch and Tate thought he found his man. He spoke up and said, "I'm looking for a man named Sublette, would that be you?"

"That'd be me, and like I said, what can I do ye fer?"

Tate introduced himself and began telling about the missionaries when Sublette stopped him with, "Now, hold on there," and reaching for his crutch, said,"foller me younker, let's step back in yonder and have us some refreshment while we talk."

As Tate explained the happenings of the past several days and the parts played by Jacques, Thumbs, and Nathan Price and the women, Sublette shook his head at the telling. "Ya know, I ain't too surprised 'bout Jacques and Thumbs, but what you're sayin' 'bout those women, that does surprise me."

"Well, after Spalding and Whitman talked about it, they thought the women, especially the younger one, were the ones that planned it all."

"Ya don't say, now if that don't beat all. An' ya' say they're on their way here?"

"They left in such a hurry, they didn't get to take much with them and they knew about the Rendezvous and were headed thisaway, comin' over Union Pass," nodding his head back the way he came. "Problem is, they've got the money box of the missionaries and I'm sure that's what they'll want to use to buy their supplies. I'm fixin' to stop 'em if I can an' get the money back to the missionaries."

"So, they're comin' o'er the pass with their wagons?" asked Sublette.

Tate grinned and nodding his head said, "Yessir, they're a pretty determined bunch."

Sublette grinned as well and said, "You got that right. They shore surprised me wit' their grit, that's for sure."

They talked more about what to do when the trio showed up and formulated a plan to confront them and retrieve the money, or at least as much of a plan as was possible, under the circumstances. Not knowing when they would arrive, or if one or all would come to the traders' tents, or what other course of action they would choose, they would have to take it as it came. Tate stood to leave and was followed out by Sublette and Lobo but was stopped as he walked around the counter when a voice hollered, "Tate! Tate Saint! Why, I'll be plumb snookered. You're the last man I expected to see up hyar!" Tate was surprised to see his friend, Kit Carson, the man that had given him his first wilderness education when he arrived at Bent's fort on his first trip to the mountains.

"Kit! Boy if you ain't a sight for sore eyes!" responded the young man of the mountains, with Lobo looking to his master with excitement, then dropped to his belly beside Tate. Although Tate towered over the well-known man by at least a handbreadth, they wrapped arms around one another and slapped each other on the back like they were best friends. Tate considered the man the elder statesman of the mountains and his mentor and teacher of all things of the wilderness and was thrilled to see this man again.

Kit leaned back and looked up at Tate and said, "What's it been, two, three years now?" then glanced down at the wolf pup and back to Tate.

"Somethin' like that, countin' the years ain't the same as rememberin' all that's happened. Seems like an eternity, all things considered," answered Tate.

"Wal, you sure have growed up since I seen you last. Why, you was still wet behind the ears then, now I cain't even reach your ears! And now look atchu, an' with a wolf pup too. I see them Comanche didn't take yore hair, Longbow, but what about any others? Any o'em try?"

"Well, I traveled a while with a fella by the name of Knuckles," and Kit interrupted him with, "Knuckles? You mean ol' Bigfist?"

"That's him. When we ran onto some Crow, I thought a woman name o' Akkeekaahuush was gonna take his hair, but she settled down after a bit. Then when we came to a Shoshone village, he was done in by a woman name o' Pinaquanáh when she introduced him to his son. So, they were happy to let me go and keep him. Other'n that, well, I guess I did have a run-in with some Arapaho, a warrior name of Little Raven and his sister, White Fawn, but that weren't nothin'. So, I guess I'm doin' O.K. so far."

When he mentioned Little Raven and White Fawn, he noticed Kit give him a questioning look, and when he finished, the mountain man said, "Little Raven and White Fawn huh? Well, you might be surprised to know they are here at Rendezvous."

"You don't say, well . . . "

"And that ain't all, White Fawn is best of friends with a

woman I kinda have my eye on, Waanibe. Maybe you an' me need to go pay a visit to those ladies, what say?"

Tate chuckled and said, "I've got to find a place to camp first, need to drop my stuff and get my horses on some grass. But, once that's done, sure."

"Problem solved, foller me and you can put your bedroll under my tent and then we'll go a visitin' tomorrow."

CHAPTER TWENTY-ONE
COURTIN'

THE FRIENDS WALKED SIDE BY SIDE, LOBO TROTTING BESIDE HIS master, as the two shared events of the past couple of years, but Tate was often distracted by the many happenings among the trappers. There were groups of men gathered around campfires, gambling, some with worn out decks of cards that were practically illegible, others used dice or other paraphernalia, anything that would elicit a bet. Even this early in the day, other groups were drinking themselves into a drunken stupor as they sought to regale one another with their exploits, both real and imagined. One group was readying a horse race while others placed their bets, and another group was gathered in a circle, betting on the outcome of a knock-down, drag-out fight between two mountain men that could easily pass for grizzly bears. Few paid attention to the passing duo, even with a wolf trotting alongside, none thinking it unusual. As they neared the encampment of the Arapaho, Tate briefly told his friend of the missionaries and the trio that robbed the group and about his plan to intercept them as they sought to buy supplies. When he mentioned Jacques and Thumbs, Kit looked at him and asked, "You did in Jacques?"

Tate nodded his head and Kit asked, "Do you know that Thumbs is here? He's been hangin' around a camp of disgruntled fur company rejects and probably up to no good. You best watch your back with that one, he won't come at you head on, he'll prob'ly get some 'o his friends to join him to try to take you down in an ambush o' some kind."

"Well, seems like there's always a hitch in the plan, ain't there. Thanks for the warnin' though," answered Tate, looking to the village of Arapaho tipis and brush huts and the many cookfires tended by the women. He thought how alike the many different tribes were, yet each maintained their own identity with clothing, language and lodges. These Arapaho reminded him of the Kiowa, but he knew better than express that, at least until he was more aware as to who were their allies and who were their enemies.

They were greeted by two warriors that recognized Carson and were directed to the lodge of Crooked Lance and his daughter, Waanibe, or Singing Grass. As they walked to the lodge, several of the people watched curiously as the two white men and the wolf pup walked among them. Two boys, each about seven or eight, stepped toward the wolf but received a warning growl and backed away. Waanibe was busy at the cookfire in front of the lodge but looked up to see the men approaching. Her broad smile told of her happiness at seeing Carson, and he held his arms wide as she walked to him to greet him with a modest embrace. Kit held her shoulders as she stood at arms-length and Carson spoke, "Waanibe, this is my friend Tate, also known as Longbow. He knows Little Raven and White Fawn. Is your friend around?"

She looked at Carson, then at Tate, and said, "Is this the man that returned White Fawn to her people?"

Carson looked at Tate, saw him drop his head as he

nodded, and then to Waanibe, "Must be, but he didn't tell me much about that."

She grinned at her friend and said, "I will go for White Fawn, she will be glad to see your friend, she has spoken much of him."

When she left, Carson looked at Tate, waiting for an explanation and Tate simply said, "Well, she was taken by a couple friends of Jacques and I sorta convinced 'em to let 'er go, thas' all," he explained as he shrugged his shoulders.

The two women hurried back to the cookfire and White Fawn had a big smile but dropped her head as she neared the fire circle, bashfully sneaking a peek at the men. Waanibe saw her reaction, giggled and spoke, "White Fawn, I'm sure you remember Longbow. Is he not the one that returned you to your people?"

White Fawn looked up at the men, and after a searching glance, dropped her eyes and answered, "Yes, this is the man. But I did not know his name." She lifted her eyes and asked, "Are you called Longbow?"

Tate was captivated by the beauty of both women, but his attention was focused on White Fawn, and he thought her more beautiful than when he saw her last. He smiled broadly and said, "Yes, I am called Longbow by many, but my other name is Tate."

Carson was watching the interaction of the two, chuckled to himself, and spoke up, "Well, how 'bout you two takin' a walk and see if you cain't get better acquainted?"

Tate looked at his friend, back at White Fawn, who nodded her head and held out her hand to the white man, offering to walk with him and show him the camp. Tate gladly accepted, motioned for Lobo to follow, and the two walked away from the fire, allowing Carson and Waanibe time together, which was exactly what Carson wanted.

Kit sat down at a willow back rest and watched as

Waanibe stirred the pot hanging over the fire, waiting for her to join him. Within moments, she was at his side and he put his arm about her and began to tell her he wanted her for his wife. She was pleased and not a little surprised, as she had many of the white trappers that tried to gain her favors, but she had rebuffed them all, even the more belligerent ones, like the French trapper, Chouinard. Waanibe and Carson talked about the necessity of gaining her father's permission, usually done by offering an acceptable bride price of trade goods, which Carson was more than willing to provide.

They were talking about plans for their future when a disturbance at the edge of the camp caught their attention. Carson stood with Waanibe at his side, when a big trapper, drunk, pushed his way through several warriors toward the two, shouting and blubbering all the way.

It was the French trapper, Chouinard. "What're ye doin' wit my woman?!" he blustered. He was a big man, standing several inches over six feet and almost as wide. His thick black beard partially obscured his neck that resembled a tree trunk, and his thick eyebrows shadowed his black piercing eyes. He was known as the 'Bully of the Mountains' and had already beaten two of his fellow Frenchmen that day. He had run rampant through the camp threatening all in his path and was especially insulting of the Americans, calling them 'crybaby school boys' and was determined to give them the spanking they deserved. Now, he was after Waanibe, believing he could bully his way through the Arapaho camp. He stood with arms out and hands spread as he looked at Waanibe and said, "You are mine, I will take you to my tent, now!"

"You ain't takin' her nowhere, Frenchy! She just agreed to be my wife!" explained Carson, who was easily outweighed by the Frenchman by at least sixty pounds and who also stood almost a foot taller than Carson.

Tate and White Fawn had returned from their walk and Tate now stepped to his friend's side, with Lobo standing, hackles raised and emitting a low growl, showing their support by pushing to the front of the crowd. Several warriors had gathered and by their position and stance, it was evident they were friends of Carson and not the Frenchman. Although he had two friends with him, if it came to a fight, he would not be on the winning side. He looked around, his friend said something to him that caused him to give the village a once-over, but his drunken state was hindering his decision making. He started to bluster again, but Carson held up his hand and said, "Frenchy, yore drunk and there's too many here. Now, you need to scram 'fore things get worse for you and your friends."

The big Frenchman staggered, caught himself, and looked at the smaller Carson through blurry eyes, "No! I come for muh woman an' I'm takin' her!" and reached out to grab Waanibe, who easily stepped away from his grasp. The Frenchman staggered forward, almost falling, until one of his friends grabbed his shirt to hold him erect. He snarled at Carson and said, "I will tear you apart you lit'le runt! If it's fight you want, we will fight!" He waved his arms around and shouted, "At the circle! Watch me tear this lil' boy apart like a leetle prairie chicken!"

Carson didn't raise his voice but looked at the man from under the brim of his hat and said, "I will rip yore guts out, Frenchy!"

The Frenchman's two companions grabbed his arms and turned him back away from the fire and with him protesting and yelling all the way, led him away from the camp.

Tate looked at his friend and asked, "Yore gonna fight that grizzly?"

Carson looked at Tate with an astounded expression and said, "Somebody's got to!"

THERE WAS ALWAYS a large open area reserved at every rendezvous, an area used for trading, fighting, dancing, or any other activity that seemed like the thing to do at the time. Word spread quickly that the 'Bully of the Mountains' was about to have another fight, but when most heard it was from the Banty Rooster of the Rockies, they were surprised, knowing the difference in size and bets were quickly being placed. Chouinard had gone to his camp, grabbed up his Hawken rifle, checked the load and cap, and swung aboard his massive mount. In any other quarters, the horse would have been thought to be a dray horse. He was a big black, long mane and tail, standing over sixteen hands and as broad of chest as the back of a wagon, with a broad back that provided a solid platform for the Frenchman to wage his fight. The two men had agreed to fight horseback, and the big man grinned knowing Carson thought it would even the odds, but he was proud of his horsemanship and like everything else, he thought he was the best. He was the first to the circle and rode around, jerking his animal about, boasting of what he was going to do, shouting down anyone that dared to argue with him. He came close to the circle of men, almost trampling those that dared to stand their ground, and waved his rifle overhead as he continued shouting his taunts to one and all.

Carson sat astride a well-muscled buckskin gelding of mustang breeding as he trotted into the circle. He had chosen a buckskin blanket held in place by a surcingle and had a single flintlock pistol tucked in his belt. It was a model 1836 built by Robert Johnson, .54 caliber smoothbore, and one he knew he could rely on, having never failed him before.

When Chouinard saw Carson, he shouted, "So, ze leetle runt came! Good for you, now you weel die!" He waved his rifle over his head as he shouted, then dug his heels into the ribs of his big black to charge at Carson. Carson waited until the two horses were about fifteen feet apart, then swung down along the neck of the buckskin as the smart-stepping gelding side passed away from the charging beast. As the animal passed, the Frenchman reined up and jerked the horse's head around, causing the animal to stumble, but he quickly caught his footing and tossed his head high with the big mane catching the wind and blowing into the face of his rider. As Carson reined the buckskin around, he heard cheering from a familiar voice and looked to see Jim Bridger, sided by Jim Beckwourth and Sublette leaning on his crutch, nodded his head to his friends and looked to the bully. Tate stood, Lobo beside him, with Waanibe and White Fawn, watching the action.

Again, the big man charged, and Carson gigged his mount forward, keeping him in line with the bigger animal, and his buckskin never faltered and a last second sidestep smashed the leg of the big man into the side of his mount, again causing a stumble. Too close to shoot, Chouinard tried to club Carson as he passed, catching nothing but air, eliciting a shout in French from the disappointed assailant. Without stopping, the Frenchman drove his horse forward to the edge of the circle, turning to bring his horse around, hoping to catch Carson from behind, but the savvy little mountain horse swiveled on his heels and rearing up slightly, dropped his front feet in a charge toward their opponent. Chouinard was determined to kill the little man and brought his rifle to his shoulder, dropped the reins to the neck of his beast and brought the muzzle down to aim at the head of Carson, but the smaller man disappeared behind the neck of the buckskin. Chouinard dropped his rifle slightly, looking for a shot at Carson, but only caught a brief glimpse of the man, under the neck of his horse, firing the flintlock directly at the face of the Frenchman. The buckskin's next step dropped the aim of the pistol just enough that the .54 caliber ball roared from the muzzle and struck Chouinard in his left hand, tore off his thumb and buried itself in the big muscled neck, severing his carotid artery.

Carson dug his heel into the side of his buckskin, pulling himself erect as the animal slid to a stop at the edge of the circle. He looked back just in time to see the man mountain tumble from the big black and plow a furrow in the dirt with his face. The horse quickly stepped aside, and the spectators seemed to hold their breath as they looked at the heap in the dirt, waiting to see movement, but there was none. Finally, someone cheered and shouted, "Yippeeee, he's done fer!"

Bridger had come alongside Carson and stood beside Tate as he looked up at the man and said, "You know, fer such a little feller, you pack a mean wallop!"

Carson looked at his pistol, down at the well-known frontiersman and said, "Ne'er known it ta' fail! I was wonderin' if you'd show up at this shebang. Didja lose yore way?"

"Nah, just took the scenic route, thas'all."

Carson invited the others to join him at his tent for some reminiscing and maybe a little drinking, introduced Tate around the circle of mountain men, and led the way to his camp. Tate took a lingering look around, rubbed Lobo behind his ears as he surveyed the crowd, hoping to see Thumbs or Price, but seeing neither, joined Carson.

The women watched as their men departed, looked to one another and started for the village. They knew the men would need their time together, it had been a valiant battle and Waanibe was proud of her man, he was great warrior. As the women talked, they were unaware of another man watching them, and planning his revenge on the young mountain man that interfered with his plans.

CHAPTER TWENTY-TWO
CLASH

SUBLETTE AND TATE LEFT THE GATHERING OF FRIENDS AT Carson's tent and walked together back to the trade counters of the company. Even now the rendezvous was starting to break up and Sublette knew by experience, it would only be two or three days more before the valley was once again surrendered to the wild. It was coming on late afternoon as they approached the trade tents and Tate was the first to see Price. The man was focused on the trade counters and rode his horse to the rail, stepping down and seeing nothing but the assorted trade goods. Tate pointed him out to Sublette and then hung back, speaking softly to Lobo to stay as he mingled with the few traders sorting their plews for the trade. Tate watched as the man bickered for his supplies and looked around to see if the women or even Thumbs were anywhere near. There was no sign of any women and Tate turned back to see Price ready to settle up for his selected goods. Tate watched as he reached into the pocket of the saddle bags hanging on his shoulder to retrieve the money.

Nathan was startled when a tomahawk whistled next to his head and buried itself in the upright pole that held the corner of the tent erect. He jumped as he looked at the hawk and turned to see from whence it came. He was shocked to see Tate standing about fifteen feet behind him, grinning.

"You weren't about to pay your bill with stolen money, were you, Price?" he said, loud enough for those nearby to hear and understand. They could tell there was something about to happen and they moved back from the two men now facing each other.

"You!" he shouted as he grabbed for his rifle, sitting against the same pole, but he snatched his hand back when Tate's Bowie twanged into the same post beside his hand.

He looked around frantically at the accusing faces of the trappers and traders, and said, "I didn't steal it! This man's the one, he killed my partners and tried to take my women!"

"And yet here you are, with all the money you stole from the missionaries," responded Tate, calmly. "And you have the brass to use their money to buy you goods for you and those women you dared to call your wife and daughter, so the three of you could run off to San Francisco. What bar did you pick them women up in, anyway?"

"Are you gonna let this man talk about my wife and daughter like that? What kind of men are you?" he whined as he looked at the gathering crowd and noticed the wolf ready to pounce.

"Tell you what, Price. Just to settle this, man to man, how 'bout you hand that money over to Sublette there, let him keep it and me'n you'll step out here an' see who's tellin' the truth. You game?" challenged Tate.

"I ain't gonna fight'chu! Why should I? I ain't done nuthin' wrong!" sniveled Price, looking around at the crowd.

Suddenly another voice came from the crowd, "He's right. That man kilt muh partner, and others too. He needs to hang!" It was Thumbs that made the accusation and Lobo turned his attention, changing his stance toward the new threat, growling and showing his teeth.

"See there! See! I tol' you, didn't I?" hollered Price.

Tate stood silently looking from Price to Thumbs and spoke slowly, "Well, there's two or three ways this can go. Either we settle it here and now, or we let Mr. Sublette speak his part, or we just wait till the missionaries get here. They'll be here, oh, probably in the mornin', don'tchu think, Price?"

"They're comin' here?" he asked, fearfully.

Tate nodded his head slowly, added a "Ummmhummm," and waited for Price's response.

The man panicked, scraped his money from the counter and grabbed at the reins of his horse, trying to mount, when Tate pulled him to the ground. He kicked back and tried to get away, but Tate simply knelt on his chest and looked at Lobo with his teeth bared within inches of the man's face and said, "I told you to let Sublette hold the money." He tugged at the saddle bags, dragging them from underneath the thief and handing them to Sublette. Without moving, he turned to scan the crowd for Thumbs, but the man had fled.

Tate stood and jerked Price to his feet and asked, "Now, where might those women be?"

"I ain't gonna tell you!" he spat.

Tate looked to Sublette and asked, "What should I do with this polecat?"

Sublette looked at the sniveling crook and said, "Shoot him, fer all I care!"

Tate reached for his Colt Paterson and cocked the hammer as he withdrew it from the holster, pushed it into the gut of Price and said to Sublette, "Here?"

"No! It'd make a mess all o'er muh stuff, take him out yonder," he said, waving his arms toward the creek in the bottom.

"No! No! Don't shoot me! I'll tell you! They're back

yonder in a camp at the tree line, there, past that pile o' rocks!"

Tate looked to Sublette again, and asked, "Now what do I do with him?"

Sublette looked at Price and thought a moment, then said, "There's a skinny juniper back behind the tent thar, sit him down an' make him hug it, and tie him off. Here, here's some rope."

He tossed the small coil of rope used for cinching down the cargo to Tate and turned back to his business, dismissing the problem with a shrug.

After securing Nathan, Tate decided he wasn't about to confront the two women by himself, so he recruited Carson to join him. When Bridger and Beckwourth heard the story, they decided to come along and see if Carson was as good at handling women as he was at besting a mountain man. The two spectators were bickering about bets as they walked behind Carson and Tate. Carson asked the younger man, "So, you say these two women were part o'the plan to steal from the missionaries?"

"That's right, an' I'ma thinkin' the younger one's the leader o' the bunch. Leastwise that's what the reverend thought. He said he saw her talkin' to Jacques and Thumbs on more'n one occasion and she seemed to be tellin' them what they was supposed to be doin'," he explained.

They arrived at the camp and caught the two women by surprise when Tate said, "Hello ladies, I see you made the trip on my horses alright." Lobo was not threatened by the women and dropped to his belly to watch.

Melissa turned and immediately assumed her innocent manner and said, "Oh, oh, I'm so glad you found us. That man, I was sure he was going to kill us. Oh, thank you, thank you," she pleaded as she slowly walked toward Tate, holding her arms out as if to embrace her deliverer.

Tate held his hands up to keep her away, turned to Carson and said, "I told you she could act."

"Oh, but Tate, please don't think that. I am glad you've come, I don't know what we would have done." She pleaded as she looked at the other men. She did a double take when she saw Bridger and turned her head away, but not before he recognized her.

Bridger chuckled, waiting to see what would happen next. He looked to Amy, thought she also looked familiar, and looked back to Carson to see if he knew the women. Tate looked to Carson and said, "I don't know what to do with 'em, do you?"

Carson chuckled and said, "Not my problem. But you did get the money back, didn't you?" At that revelation, the women looked at Tate, and Melissa squinted her eyes at the young man but caught herself, and started to make another plea but was stopped by Bridger, when he said to Carson, "Did you say they tried to lift the poke o' some missionaries?"

"That's what Tate said," answered Carson, looking at Tate for an explanation.

"Yup, they'll be along, probably tomorrow, but these two an' a fella that I got tied up behind Sublette's, planned to massacre the whole bunch an' take their money an' run off to San Francisco."

"That's about right. That 'un," said Bridger and pointed at Melissa, "lifted my poke when I was in Liberty las' time. 'course I had too much to drink, but I shore 'member her, you betcha!" He looked to Amy and said, "An' that'n looks familiar too, prob'ly worked in the same joint."

"But what do we do with 'em now?" asked Tate.

"Wal, I'm sure there's any number o' fellas'd like to take 'em to their cabins fer the winter, but I don't think these two'd make it till greenup. Mebbe we can git Sublette to take 'em back to St. Louie wid him, just ta' git 'em outta th' mountains," suggested Bechwourth, grinning at the women.

"Well, we can't trust 'em to let 'em go. They'd probably find somebody else to do their killin' for 'em and won't nobody be safe. Personally, I'd rather have a grizzly bear for a pet, than these two," declared Carson.

When the idea, with ladies in tow, was presented to Sublette, he wasn't too agreeable, but when Fitzpatrick chimed in with, "We can't leave 'em here, Bill. I'll let 'em ride in my wagon with me. I'm sure they'll be alright, won't you ladies?" Both readily agreed and promised to be on their best behavior and work to earn their way, Sublette begrudgingly agreed with the condition that Fitzpatrick would be responsible. He grinned at his partner, smiled at the ladies, and sent them away to fetch their belongings to ready themselves for the return trip to St. Louis.

Tate left the others and walked around the tent to retrieve his other problem that he left tied to the tree but was surprised to find nothing but a cut rope and assorted tracks around the juniper trunk. He looked about, saw nothing and returned to tell Sublette. "That Price fella, I'm thinkin' Thumbs cut him loose. So, you hang onto that saddle bag with the missionaries' money an' I'll start lookin' for them."

Tate found the others at Carson's camp, told them about Price and they all agreed with Carson when he said, "If he's with Thumbs, there's no tellin' where they'll be, maybe even left the country. Since you got the money back, easiest thing ta' do is leave sleepin' dogs lie."

"You're probably right, 'sides, I ain't in the retribution business, anyhow," grumbled Tate.

The other men made their excuses, and Carson suggested to Tate that the two of them return to the Arapaho camp and finish what they started earlier. Tate grinned at his friend and asked, "Did you really ask Waanibe to be your wife?"

"Shore did. She's a purty one, ain't she?" he replied.

"Yup, she is, but, married an' settlin' down, I dunno."

"Who said anything 'bout settlin' down? That's the difference with a Indian woman, they expect to go wherever their man goes. I ain't settlin' down, just takin' a wife with me!" declared Carson.

Tate looked at his friend, thinking about what he said, and began to consider the possibilities. He enjoyed his solitude, but there were times . . . well, times when it would be nice to have company and White Fawn was the prettiest woman he had ever seen. He reached down and stroked the neck of Lobo and asked, "What do you think, Lobo? Do we need any company, what with winter comin' on all too soon?" The wolf looked at Tate with mouth open and tongue lolling to the side and cocked his head with a little whine as if asking a question or voicing his 'I don't care' opinion. Tate shook his head and said, "You're no help."

CHAPTER TWENTY-THREE
SEPARATION

After talking with Carson about the traditions of the Arapaho and his agreed upon bride price for Waanibe, Tate decided to cover all possibilities and went to Sublette. The trader was ramrodding his crew as they began tearing down the trade tents and loading the many plews that were the last of the trades. Tate interrupted his friend and began to finagle a trade with the man, and as he began to list the goods he wanted, Sublette looked at him and asked, "Are you startin' a war or sumpin'? Let's see here, two trade fusils, one new Hawken, powder an' lead, blankets, just whatchu up to younker?"

When Tate told him about the possibility of taking an Arapaho for a wife, the trader grinned, "Is that the one I saw you standin' with, the one with Carson's woman?"

Tate dropped his head, nodded, and looked back at the man who stood grinning. Sublette said, "Well, then, if yore tradin' fer a woman, you need sumpin' else." He walked to the back of the counter and brought out a couple of exceptionally crafted skinning knives and sheaths. "Now, if you cain't buy a bride with all that plunder, you need to stick wit' yore wolf thar and be content with him to warm yore feet in the winter time."

Tate settled up, paying in gold coin taken from the special pockets in his belt, and gathered his take and lashed the goods to his pack horse and started for his camp, Lobo beside him. He looked back to Sublette and asked, "You ain't leavin' till in the mornin' are ya? I wanna make sure them missionaries get here in time to resupply, if'n that's alright."

"I'll be here, an I'll keep some stuff aside that they'll prob'ly want," answered Sublette as he waved to his friend. Tate had walked just a short way from the trade tents when he saw the wagons coming down the trail from the northern mountains. He immediately recognized the three wagons as those of the missionaries and grinned at the sight. He found himself a seat on a nearby pile of rocks and waited as the wagons approached. He waved at the group and stood as they drew near.

"Well, I'm glad to see you folks. I see you made it alright, any trouble?" he asked.

The reverend reined up the team, stopping the wagons and wrapped the reins around the brake handle before he answered the inquiry. He grinned at Tate as he said, "Nothing out of sorts, you?"

"Oh, nothing out of sorts. Before you step down, you might want to direct the rest of the wagons to pull up over yonder," pointing to an area near the stream that still had a little graze remaining, "but you might wanna make your way to the tradin' tents, o'er thar. Sublette is packin' up an' you might wanna resupply while yore still able. Also, he's got your money waitin' for you."

The missionary smiled at the report of the retrieved the money and asked, "And the three that took it?"

"Wal, Thumbs and Price are on the run, but the women

folks are in the company of Fitzpatrick and he's gonna take 'em back to the city."

"And nothing will be done about their thievery?" inquired the missionary.

"Well, since we don't have any 'official' law out here, an' no jail to put anybody in, most agreed it to be best just to be rid of 'em."

"I understand," replied the somber man, looking down at the footboard of the wagon. He lifted his eyes back to Tate and said, "I guess that's best. And as Christians, I reckon we should forgive them."

Tate grinned at the thought and added, "Uh, I reckon that's 'tween you an' the Lord. As fer me, well . . ." and he let the thought linger without resolving the issue. "I'll be along this evenin' to get the rest of muh gear an' animals, if'n that's alright?"

"Of course, and I'm sure the others would like to thank you for retrieving our funds. It is certainly an answer to prayer. You have lived up to your name, sir."

Tate frowned at the remark, not understanding, and upon seeing his expression, the missionary explained, "Saint, you have proven yourself to be a Saint for all you've done for us, and we are eternally grateful. We would not have been able to continue our mission work had you not retrieved our funds. Thank you again."

Tate nodded his head and waved off the praise as he walked around the wagon to return to his camp and his friend, with Lobo trailing at his side. He was greeted by Carson, who was busy assembling an assortment of trade goods and other items, apparently readying his bride price for the father of Waanibe, Crooked Lance. The image before Tate turned his mind once again to White Fawn. Each time he thought of her or pictured her image, he felt a warmness in his spirit that he had never experienced before. He had examined his feelings ever since Carson had first spoken of taking Waanibe as his bride. He realized the young woman had never been out of his thoughts from the first time he saw her in the company of her two captors. And the smile she gave him when he sent her back to her people told him she had thought fondly of him as well, and when Waanibe said the girl had often spoken of him, he was surprisingly pleased and warmed at the thought. But was he thinking of taking her as his wife just because his mentor and friend was taking a wife? Was he simply considering such action to follow the steps and example of his friend? As he pondered these questions, he set his own mind at ease when he reflected on the thoughts he treasured from the first moment he met this woman, those feelings had filled his mind and heart long before any conversation or suggestion by his friend. When he watched her ride away that first time, his heart sunk, and he began wondering if he would ever see her again. Now, all he could think of was that he did not want to be separated from this woman again; any future without her promised nothing but darkness and loneliness. Just the thought of her painted a smile on his face and gave everything around him a special meaning. Yes, he wanted this woman by his side and he was certain she felt the same way, but he would not know for sure until he spoke to Little Raven about White Fawn.

Carson had casually watched his friend while he readied his packet. He stood and looked at Tate and said, "You look like a pup that's lost his best friend. Thinkin' 'bout White Fawn are ye?"

Tate lifted his eyes to his mentor and said, "Yeah, I was, so, what do I do now?"

"You got you a bride price gathered up?"

Tate looked at Carson, chuckling, and shaking his head, replied, "Yup, I guess I did."

"Wal then, gather it up an' come on along, le's go git us a

bride!" he declared, laughing at his young friend, watching him turn red from the neck up.

Tate asked Carson for patience while he returned to the missionaries to retrieve his other horses and gear. It was just a short while later when the young man came riding up to Carson's camp, leading a loaded pack horse and trailing three others. He had also fetched the two horses stolen by the women and planned on adding them to the gifts for Little Raven as the bride price for White Fawn. The two suitors soon had everything gathered and loaded and were headed for the Arapaho encampment. On the way, Carson explained to Tate the tradition and practice of the Arapaho, or as they referred to themselves, Hinono'eino, the people, regarding the joining of two as one. Tate listened intently, nodding in understanding and with no questions, then the two separated, Carson to the lodge of Crooked Lance and Tate to the lodge of Little Raven.

Initially, Tate thought he and his friend moved through the village drawing little attention. But to the many people busy about their usual duties, it was apparent what the intentions of the two men were. And as the people watched, their curiosity prompted both cheers and jeers, all in good fun, but much to the embarrassment of Tate.

As he neared the lodge of Little Raven, he saw White Fawn look at him and flash a smile as she ducked her head into the lodge to tell Little Raven of the coming of the white man. When Little Raven came from his lodge, he was purposefully stoic and even stern in his expression as the man approached his fire. When Tate raised his hand, and greeted the brother of White Fawn with, "A-Ho, Little Raven," he received a nod from the man that stood with a blanket over one shoulder, and long fur tufted braids hanging over his shoulders. Little Raven looked at the horses led by Tate and the large pack on one, looked back at Tate and asked, "Why do you come to my lodge?"

"I bring gifts to you to show my desire to take your sister as my woman," he explained, trying to remember exactly how Carson had instructed him, hoping he had it right.

Little Raven waved his free hand in a sweeping motion, indicating to Tate to spread his gifts on the ground before him. Without speaking, Tate turned and began loosening the large pack from the first horse. Sitting it on the ground, he untied the binds and spread the first blanket on the ground at the feet of Little Raven. Then carefully and with somewhat exaggerated motions, he lay the folded extra blankets, the two fusil trade rifles, the powder and lead, and finally the treasured Hawken rifle. Several of the villagers had gathered to witness this exchange and when the Hawken was presented, a murmur arose among the people, knowing this was an exceptional gift. Tate dropped the leads of the two horses and motioned toward them to indicate they were also a part of the gifts, then stepped back to await Little Raven's response.

The brother, having assumed the position and responsibility of the leadership of the family when their father was killed on a raid into Blackfoot country, took this honor very seriously, knowing the importance of the life and happiness of his sister. The people of the village knew that one day Little Raven would be a leader of their people and everything he did, even this giving of his sister, would be watched by everyone. He walked to the horses, looked them over, touching them and looking at their teeth to determine their age, then to their hooves and giving them a fair inspection. Then he went to the blanket and knelt down to examine the offering. He looked at the blankets, the trade fusils, and finally lifted the Hawken, handling it with care and respect. No one in his village had such a fine rifle as this Hawken and his expression showed he was pleased. He sat the rifle back on the blanket and stood, looked at Tate and motioned for him to come into his lodge. As Little Raven disappeared into the lodge, that signified acceptance of this man as a mate for White Fawn.

Although she had stayed behind the lodge during this presentation, when her brother went into the tipi, she ran to her friends and they happily shared her joy. Several women gathered around White Fawn and began chattering about the preparations that must begin immediately, one older woman placed an arm around her shoulders and began steering her toward her lodge. The women would prepare the dress for the girl, and the older women would give their counsel and advice during the process. Others would prepare a separate lodge for the couple to have to themselves for the first night after the joining, then they would have to prepare their own lodge with hides donated and taken by the man who would be her mate.

As Tate entered the tipi of Little Raven, he was followed by several of the elders of the village. Their part was to speak with this man that would become one of them by joining together with White Fawn and provide advice and counsel as to the ways of the Hinono'eino. They knew he would take the woman from their village, but both would still be considered a part of this village and the people, and as such, must learn to conduct themselves in accordance with the way of the people. The next day would be devoted to the giving of gifts from the woman's family to Tate and the joining ceremony. When the counselors asked about Carson and his plans, they agreed it would be a special ceremony to have both couples joined together. Tate readily agreed and was told to get the rest of his gear together and he and Carson were to come back to spend the night in the village.

Tate had no sooner exited the lodge and he saw Carson

walking toward him. The two men greeted one another, exchanging congratulations and enjoying the moment together. Tate asked Carson, "So, why are we supposed to stay in the village?"

"Well, they're probably preparing a sweat lodge for us, an' we'll need to have a cleansing to prepare us for the big day. E'er had a time in a sweat lodge?" he asked his young friend. Tate shook his head and said, "Only if you call spendin' a summer in the woods in Missouri a sweat lodge."

Carson slapped his friend on the back and said, "Actually, it ain't bad. You'll prob'ly like it!"

CHAPTER TWENTY-FOUR
TAKEN

White Fawn lay on her stomach, tied and gagged, across the rump of his horse as Thumbs rode back into their camp. Nathan Price stood, coffee cup in hand, staring at the parcel behind the cantle of Thumbs saddle. It was the middle of the night and he was expecting his partner to return from a last effort at resupplying before they took off for the high and lonesome. He looked to Thumbs as he swung a leg over his saddle and parcel, and bellowed, "What have you done! Are you crazy?! You're gonna have the whole tribe after us!"

"Ahh, they don't even know she's gone! An' they won't till mornin' an' we'll be long gone by then. 'Sides, this here's the woman Tate wanted, he was makin' a deal to take her as his woman an' they was gettin' her ready. They jus' din't know they was gittin' her ready fer us!" He cackled as he pulled her off the horse, letting her drop to the ground unaided. She rolled in the dirt, tried to kick at Thumbs and got kicked in return. Price, surprised at the turn of events and the new burden, looked at Thumbs and said, "That's all we need. You kickin' and beatin' on her and when the Injuns catch up to us, they'll give us worse!"

"Ha, it ain't gonna be the Injuns that'll be comin', it's gonna be that snot-nosed punk what done in our friends, an' I'm gonna fix him when he shows up. Everything we do to her's gonna hurt him worse'n anything we do ta' him, an' I'm gonna enjoy it more, yessirree I am!"

Price shook his head and started gathering things together as he snarled back at Thumbs, "Well, 'fore you go gettin' any ideas, we need to clear outta here, put some miles behind us 'fore they come stormin' down on us!"

Thumbs kicked some dirt on the coals and grumbled, "Alright, alright, mebbe yore right. 'sides, it'll give us more time after we're outta this country."

With only two horses, the woman would have to ride with one of the men and when Thumbs insisted, Price convinced him to untie her ankles and let her ride astraddle. He begrudgingly agreed, untied her and lifted her atop his mount, seating her on his bedroll directly behind the cantle. By the time they were ready to leave camp, the first light of dawn was showing in the east, and the men started on the trail that would follow the Green River downstream.

THE SWEAT LODGE was an experience for Tate, not quite knowing what to expect but knowing the name alone told much. It was bad enough to sit and sweat but listening to the chanting of the two elders that shared the lodge with him and Carson, just added to the discomfort. When the two grey-headed men crawled from the dark canopy of the sweat lodge, Carson and Tate willingly followed, but when they were told to follow with nothing but a blanket wrapped around them, Tate and Carson winced as they walked bare-foot on the rocky trail to the trees. When the old men set the example by dropping the blankets and taking a running jump into the snowmelt runoff water of the Green River, Tate hesitated, but followed and was surprised at the sudden cold water and the stimulating effect on his hot tired body. But none of the men spent too long in the running cold water and all four were soon trudging to their lodges and the waiting warm fire and buffalo robes.

With the coming of first light, both Carson and Tate were up and dressing in their ceremonial garb, provided by the families of the brides. The buckskins were well made, lightly decorated with beads and quills, each in a particular pattern, with beautiful work and craftsmanship. While Carson's were a darker brown, almost red, Tate's were a very light gold tone. The men were finishing their dressing when the entry flap was suddenly flipped aside, and Little Raven stepped in, visibly upset. He looked at the men and directed himself to Tate, "White Fawn has been taken!"

Tate was stunned, and asked, "What do you mean, taken?"

"Sometime in the night, someone, probably a white man, took her from the ceremonial lodge. She was there by herself, preparing for this day. When the women went for her, she was gone! She did not leave willingly, the flap had been cut, and she is without moccasins."

"Then let's go get her!" demanded Tate, reaching for his Hawken and other gear. He looked to Carson and said, "Probably that Thumbs and Price, wantin' to get back at me!"

"You're probably right, ain't no one else dumb 'nuff to go 'gainst the whole Arapaho tribe. Hang on, an' I'll go wit'chu!" he stated.

"No, you've got a bride to 'tend to, I'm sure Little Raven'll be wantin' to go too. I'd be obliged if'n you watch o'er muh stuff, or cache it somewhere, till I git back. I'm takin' two horses, no packs, just movin' fast."

"Good idea. I'll take care o' yer stuff, an' me'n Waanibe won't be goin' nowheres any time soon."

Tate nodded as he ducked through the entry, surprised to

see his grulla and the black held by a young boy, waiting for him. He quickly saddled the grulla, stuffed the Hawken in the scabbard, finished with his belt and other accouterments, and was stepping in the stirrup when Little Raven reined up beside him, also leading a second mount. The man was attired in buckskins, with two feathers, nocked and painted, dangling at the back of his head. He held his new Hawken across the withers of his mount and sported the powder horn and possibles bag hanging across his chest. He had a quiver of arrows at his back and an unstrung bow protruded from the top of the quiver. He looked at Tate's quiver that hung from the pommel of his saddle and saw the tip of the longbow extending past the butt of the Hawken. He nodded at the white man and without speaking, led off to the trail and the tracks of the horse that carried White Fawn.

As they left the village, Little Raven was lying low on the neck of his mount, examining the tracks as they rode at a trot. He lifted up, looking along the trees at the edge of the river, and dug heels into the ribs of his rangy appaloosa. Tate followed close on his heels, as the four horses stretched out into a full ground eating gallop. Although Tate had become an excellent tracker and could hold his own with anyone, he willingly yielded to Little Raven and his knowledge of the country.

Raven knew horses and would drop from a gallop to a canter to a walk, letting the horses catch their wind and cool off and giving him the opportunity to check the sign. Tate would use that time to put Lobo up behind him, letting him get some rest as well. Occasionally, Raven would lean down far enough, holding to the mane of his mount and with his heel hooked, to practically touch the tracks. Tate watched as the man effortlessly pulled himself erect and looked back to nod to Tate, to assure him they were still on the trail. By late morning Raven pointed the appaloosa to the trees by the riverbank and gaining the shade from a pair of crooked cottonwoods, he dropped to the ground and let the horses go to the water and begin to graze. Tate joined him, Lobo at his side, by the rough barked trees, stepping over the bare log of a long dead cottonwood, and said to Raven, "Two horses, one carrying double, so must be two men and one with White Fawn, right?"

"Yes, you read sign well. They are not traveling fast, but they are moving steady. We are maybe," and he held his closed palm to the sun, "two hands behind." Tate knew the measurement of extended hand-widths was close to the measurement of an hour. He looked at the sun, the terrain before them and said, "Then we should catch them by dark?"

Raven looked at Tate, slowly nodded his head, approving of the white man and his knowledge of the wild. He glanced down at the tomahawk in Tate's belt and bent his head to the side to look at it a little better when Tate drew it from his belt and handed it to him. He said, "Look it over, I'm gettin' us some pemmican and a couple biscuits." Raven held the tomahawk almost reverently, recognizing it as a thing of beauty and great craftsmanship. When he realized it was also a pipe, he looked toward Tate and back at the hawk, because the keeper of the pipe among the Arapaho is thought to be a holy man. As he continued to examine the hawk, he moved his fingers over the carving of the eagle's wings, the bead-work by the head, and hefted the hawk to feel it's weight and balance. When Tate returned he looked at the man and said, "This is a magnificent weapon, did you make it?"

Tate chuckled and said, "No, no, that was a gift from a chief of the Osage, Black Buffalo."

"Osage, I do not know the Osage."

"They are a fine people, very tall," he motioned with his hand above his head, "but good people. They live far to the south and east. Black Buffalo is a great leader."

Little Raven knew it was considered bad manners to ask about the reason for the gift so he did not, but his curiosity caused him to look at this man that would have his sister to join with and knew there was more to this man than he first thought. To receive a gift of this worth and from a chief of a people was indeed an honor and one not lightly given by any people. Their short rest over, the two were soon on the trail again and kicked the new mounts into a gallop, trailing the others behind. Tate looked at the sun, calculated it to be approaching midday. He looked at the rolling plains before them, knowing their mounts, relaying as they were, would be able to gain ground on the kidnappers. He, for the first time, filled his mind with thoughts of White Fawn, gritting his teeth in anger at her captors, vowing to himself that Thumbs and Price would not get another chance to do wrong to anyone.

CHAPTER TWENTY-FIVE
CHASE

"Easy now," whispered Thumbs, looking to Price who rode almost alongside but slightly behind, "we don' wanna spook 'em." Thumbs was sitting easy on his mount, keeping the nervous animal to a walk, as they watched the herd of buffalo coming from the riverside. Easily more than a thousand of the woolies, the herd was moving north for greener grass and their easy gait and lumbering heads were deceiving as to their strength, especially if they were spooked. Thumbs had witnessed the destruction left in the path of a stampeding herd of buffalo and he knew if anything were to spook the herd, they would not have any chance of escape. He leaned over the neck of his horse, patting the animal on his neck and talking softly to him. Even with this massive herd, the dust cloud was minimal, due to a recent cloudburst that covered the plains with just enough water to settle the powdery soil. But by the time the end of the herd trampled all the moisture into the ground, a thin cloud of dust rose behind them.

Price had never seen a herd of buffalo and he was mesmerized by the massive herd and the lumbering beasts with the bulls standing well over six feet at the hump and weighing close to a ton, they were impressive animals and sent a shiver of fear through the easterner. "Shouldn't we move faster, get past 'em 'fore they get too close," he whispered, his eyes wide, showing more white than color. He gripped the reins tight in his white-knuckled hands and nervously twisted in his seat, looking all around, fearful of seeing a charging woolie storming down on him.

"Take it easy! When we get past 'em, they'll wipe out our trail an' we'll be rid o' whoever's follerin' us. Just be quiet and move slow, just like me," directed Thumbs. Price nodded at his partner, but fretfully watched the approaching brown tide. He leaned on his pommel, trying to steady his shaking hands, and dropped one of the reins that fell loosely and began to drag and causing the man to holler, "No!" The horse stepped on the rein, stumbled, and Price grabbed at the saddle horn as he fought for his balance, looking frantically at Thumbs and said loudly, "Help me! I lost the rein!" panic evident in his voice.

Whether it was the noise from the men, the nervous prancing of the horses, the panicked cry from Price, there was no way of knowing. But the buffalo lunged as if they were all joined together and the brown rolling plain of buffalo humps became a seething tide of stampeding animals. Thumbs saw the jump of the herd and immediately dug his heels into the ribs of his horse, with one hand on the reins and the other reaching behind to hold to the tunic of White Fawn. The horse leaped into a gallop, and with more sense than either of his riders, he knew the danger they were in and dug his hooves to fight his way across the undulating plains. Thumbs lay his face into the horse's mane, slapping leather continuously and hollering to his mount, "Faster, faster, faster!"

Price's horse sought to follow that of Thumbs but stumbled again on the rein that jerked his head down, pulling at the bit in his mouth. He started to turn in a tight circle, trying to escape the rein that seemed to tie him down, then he started bucking and rearing, dropped to all fours and finally found footing to chase after the other horse. The thunder of the herd, bellowing and grunting with every step with each footfall adding to the rumble, they roared across the flats. What had been a wispy thin dust cloud now became a brown specter that threatened the breath of every living creature. Unseen in the melee, rabbits scurried for holes, coyotes tucked tails and ran helter skelter seeking any protection from the brown mass of destruction that shook the very earth they traveled and joined the rabbits in their holes. The herd covered the flats like a great wave, with each move of the leaders the entire horde moved as if choreographed by some unseen entity, and still they thundered on. Sagebrush, cactus, prairie dog towns, rock formations, all blended together in the plowed under and churned up dirt leaving a broad path of dark turned soil behind.

The cloud of dust enveloped Thumbs and White Fawn, the horse was showing lather and began to falter in his step, but Thumbs could see the edge of the cloud just before them and slapped leather again, shouting at his horse, "Come on you crowbait! Move it! We can make it, come on, dig!" The shouts of the terrified man could not be heard by the horse, with ears just a couple of feet from the screams of the man. The thunder of the herd drowned out every semblance of noise that fought against the maelstrom of sound.

But suddenly they were free of the path of the herd and Thumbs dared to look back to see the herd continue on their path of destruction, with a few cows and calves lagging behind. He reined up on the horse, let it walk for a short distance, and believing them safe, Thumbs reined the horse toward a cluster of juniper and nearby sage. He gave White

Fawn a hand down and before he stepped from his mount, he stood in the stirrups to see if there was any sign of Price. The man was nowhere to be seen.

"Guess he didn't make it!" he said to White Fawn as he dropped to the ground, slowly making his way to a moss-covered boulder with a cholla growing nearby. He sat down, leaned back and lay prone on the stone, looking skyward, watching the brown cloud slowly dissipate. He looked at White Fawn, sitting in the shade of the Juniper, hands still tied, as she dropped her head to her knees, breathing heavily.

The continued effort to stay aboard the horse with nothing to keep her on but the grip of her legs had exhausted her. Several times she was certain she would be lost in the stampede, but each time she managed to hang on and now she wondered why she hadn't let her life end with the stampede. She was hopeful that Tate would come for her, and maybe Little Raven also, but with the herd destroying their trail, would they be able to find her? And would they find her before this man destroyed her? With her head bowed and forehead resting on her knees, she prayed, *Oh, great Be He Teiht, Creator of all, give my brother and my man sight to see the trail and strength to follow. Let them take me from this man or give me strength to escape.* She lifted her head and saw Thumbs staring at her and she dropped her head again, not wanting to see him ogling her.

LITTLE RAVEN HAD SLOWED their pace to a steady canter and Tate moved alongside, seeking to see the tracks and sign of those before them. Little Raven pointed to the southern horizon and the slowly lifting thin cloud of dust. Tate looked in the direction of the cloud, back to Little Raven and said, "You don't think that's them, do ya'?"

"No, I think it is too far and made by something else. Maybe buffalo."

"Buffalo steak'd taste mighty fine, but we ain't got time to go after 'em."

"After. On our way home, we take buffalo," said Raven, grinning in anticipation.

Tate nodded his head, understanding and agreeing. It would be good to take back some buffalo. *Make a good wedding supper,* he thought, grinning.

They crossed a shallow gravelly bottomed stream that fed the Green and were following the trail in the dry land above the wide river bottom. The broad bottomland of the Green had a myriad of marshes, ponds, and twisting stream beds, apparently only flowing when the snow melt was sufficient. Now, the sub-irrigated ground held promises of bogs and quicksand. The tracks and sign of the captors held to the dry land above the river and so too did the pursuers.

Raven slowed the pace to a walk, giving Lobo a chance to catch up and letting Tate drop to the ground to help the growing wolf-pup to his seat behind his saddle. Shady and Lobo were becoming fast friends and when apart, they could be found looking for each other. Lobo would usually lay in the grass near Shady as the grulla grazed, or beside Tate wherever he tended to his duties in camp or snoozed in the shade. Lobo would not be far from his master as the two had become inseparable.

Raven shook his head in amazement at this white man that kept a wolf at his side and allowed the wolf to ride on his horse. Both men were walking and leading their mounts, giving the animals a time to cool off and regain their wind, when they felt the ground begin to vibrate. Both froze, looking around the immediate vicinity and seeing nothing, and began to look in the distance. A distant rumble that made them first think of a coming thunderstorm, came from the south. But the only cloud to be seen was the rising dust cloud viewed earlier.

All the horses had stopped, lifted their heads with ears forward and eyes searching for the commotion. Both men mounted, and Tate stood in his stirrups to look in the distance, he reached back to his saddle bags and withdrew the spyglass and put it to his eye to search the distant plains. His eyes grew wide as the line of dark brown moved and the cloud billowed. He looked for a moment longer, handed the glass to Raven and said, "I think it's a herd o' buffalo. I'm thinkin' they're stampedin'!"

Raven looked through the glass, turned to Tate to hand it back to him and said, "Yes, and Fawn is between us and the buffalo!"

Raven and Tate slapped leather, kicking their mounts to a full out run. The prairie land dipped and rose with dry gulches and washes, alkali flats, and cactus patches. Raven gave his mount his head, hanging on as the horse masterfully maneuvered between the obstacles. Tate's concern was for a chuck hole or a prairie dog town that would snap a horse's leg in an instant. But he trailed the Indian and gave no ground. Suddenly, Raven pulled his mount to a sliding stop as the men saw the brown tide crest a far rise, coming directly toward them.

The wafting dust cloud rose like a giant curtain, masking the bulk of the herd, but Raven knew this was a stampede to avoid at all costs. He frantically searched the area and seeing nothing for cover, he jerked the head of his horse around and pointed him to the bank of the Green River. The horses dug in their hooves as they scampered for the cover of the river flats and the inviting trees. As they neared the bank, Raven saw the drop off to the river below, but gigged his horse on and they dropped over the rim and with Raven laying back on the rump of his horse, they slid down to the river below.

Tate followed and as he leaned back, he pinned the wolf to the rump of Shady as the grulla dropped his butt to the loose sand with the black chasing and they slid all the way to the bottom. When they hit the grassy flats, Raven kept going until they came to river's edge and the scattering of cottonwood and larch. He looked back, seeing only the rising cloud of dust trailing after the stampede.

Raven slid from his horse, led both animals to the water, sided by Tate and his animals and the men dropped to their bellies to suck deep in the water. Lobo lapped water beside Tate and looked up at the man as if he thought what they just did was fun, and he was ready to go again. Tate shook his head at the wolf, looked to Raven as both men sat back on the grassy bank and said, "I thought you wanted some buffalo steak." Raven looked at his friend, shook his head and grinned at the thought of taking a buffalo during a stampede. Only a white man would think such a thing.

CHAPTER TWENTY-SIX
HUNT

THUMBS LOOKED AT WHITE FAWN, PULLED HIS HAT OVER HIS eyes and with hands behind his head, pretended to drop off to sleep, just to see what the woman would do. Through narrow slits, he watched her from the corner of his eye as she leaned back against the dry bark of the juniper to rest. She sat motionless.

Having leaned her head back and closed her eyes she appeared to be snoozing. Her breathing was slow and even and she had let her head tilt to the side where she could watch the man from underneath long unmoving eyelashes. She knew this man was not sleeping, he was too restless, and his breathing was uneven, and she believed he was watching her, waiting for a reason to attack her, but she would not yield.

Finally, Thumbs was the first to move, lifting his hat and sitting up, to survey the area around their slight promontory. He stood, hitching up his britches, and looked in the direction of the disappearing herd of buffalo. The brown beasts had continued their stampede for a considerable distance, but also followed the smaller fork that fed the Green River and had slowed their progress. Apparently tired and hungry, the brown mass seemed to have stopped and were milling around. Even though the animals were at least three or four miles distant, the herd lay like a dark woolly blanket across the dry terrain. He looked over the churned soil that marked the herd's passage and lifted his eyes beyond to the western mountains, then turned to look at the flats to the south and east and the far mountains behind him. He considered his predicament, those following, whoever they were and how many he did not know but he wasn't anxious to be caught by them and decided to cut back across the path of the stampede and cross the Green River and make for the nearer mountains. He looked just below them and mentally mapped their course, using a dry gulch that would keep them from view and believing their tracks would be hard to find in the freshly churned soil.

He looked to White Fawn and barked, "Come on woman! We're makin' tracks!"

She struggled to her feet to follow after the man as he picked up the reins of the horse and started walking from the slight rise that had been their temporary island of refuge. As she turned away from the juniper, she broke a branch, pointing the broken end in the direction they were headed. When the man turned, she acted like she had stumbled and grabbed the branch to catch herself, then stepped toward him as if obediently following.

Within moments, they were in the shallow draw, and finding the footing in the loose soil difficult, Thumbs mounted up but made Fawn walk in front of the horse, taking a perverse pleasure out of bumping the sweaty animal against her every time she slowed her pace. He was more intent on his agitating of the woman than he was regarding his own progress and failed to look behind him to see the very visible trial their deep prints were making in the soft soil.

It was a short break taken by Little Raven and Tate, but enough of one for the horses to be cooled down, watered and fed, and the men mounted up to continue their hunt for White Fawn and her captors. They angled across the face of the sandy slope that led from the river bottom and as they crested, Raven stopped to look over the sign of the passing herd. For a width of over two hundred yards, the fresh turned soil from the stampeding herd tattooed the landscape from beyond the southern horizon to three or more miles to the north east. He could see the slowly settling brown dust cloud and the dark line in the east that would be the herd, apparently stopped for water and graze. He looked at Tate and said, "No, we are not going after the buffalo."

Tate grinned, knowing that Raven knew he did not want to go after buffalo, but only to find White Fawn. When Raven gigged his mount forward, jerking the lead line on his spare mount tight, Lobo trotted off ahead to be followed by Tate and the led black. As they rode, they continuously looked at the turned-up soil, searching for any sign of the passing of the abductors. Raven motioned for Tate to swing wide and when about thirty yards distant, he reined his horse so his path would parallel that of Raven's. Both men scanned the soil, occasionally lifting their eyes to look farther in both directions, but mostly searching left and right about fifteen yards on either side.

After traversing about one hundred fifty yards of the buffalo's path, something fluttering in the slight breeze caught Tate's eye. He stopped, looked and reined his horse toward the fluttering object. As he neared, he saw a disturbing sight. The leather from a stirrup and fender of a saddle protruded up from the churned soil, a little further was another piece, this one from the cantle of the saddle and next to it, partially buried in the soil was the bottom of a man's boot. He whistled for Raven's attention and motioned the man to join him. Tate dropped from his saddle, ground tied his horse, and walked slowly in a meandering manner, searching for any other sign. Raven saw the same things as Tate and he also began searching on foot. Both men were afraid of finding White Fawn, but after a reasonable search, all that was found was more evidence of one man and one horse. When a portion of a shirt was found, Tate recognized it. "This was Price's shirt, so this must be him. I'm thinkin' he's the only one here, at least so far."

"Let's circle back a little, look wider, be sure," tersely instructed Raven. Tate nodded his head and swung aboard the grulla to continue. As their search proved unproductive, Raven looked back to where they lost the trail as it entered the path of the stampede, turned to look beyond the path along the same line, and pointed for them to go in that direction. When they left the churned soil path, Raven motioned he would go to the left along the edge of the wide path and Tate was to go to the right, each looking for where the other captor left the trail. Within moments, Raven gave a clear imitation of a night hawk that caught Tate's attention, and following the hand signals of the man, they both started in the direction of the scattered juniper well away from the stampede trail. They were moving at a canter and quickly joined one another as Raven pointed to the tracks, clearly leading to the rocky knoll beside the juniper, but there was little cover and they did not expect to see Thumbs and his captive there.

Tate brought the grulla to a sudden stop and followed Lobo to the flat boulder atop the knoll and seeing nothing, began searching for any sign. He saw the tracks where the horse dug around for some graze, cropped a couple clumps of bunch grass, and then he saw the sign where someone had sat next to the tree. He turned to look at Raven who was standing on the flat boulder, and saw the broken branch, obviously bent to give a sign. "Raven!" he called and pointed at the branch, prompting Raven to quickly come to his side.

As the men looked at the branch and the tracks in the soil and dried needles, Raven looked to Tate and said, "She has told us, they go in that direction," he said as he pointed toward the dry gulch leading back to the Green.

Both men quickly mounted and started toward the gulch, Raven leaning down to read the sign. He turned to see if Tate had also seen the tracks of small moccasins and larger boots. When the sign showed the man was riding and the woman still walking, it was evident that the horse had hit the woman, causing her to stumble and catch herself with her hands, undoubtedly bound together. Raven was sure the stumble had been Fawn's way of showing her brother she was bound, and he grinned at the canny ways of his sister.

Suddenly a faint scream sounded from well ahead of them, and judging by the sound and the slight echo, Raven judged it came from below the banks of the Green River. He turned quickly to see Tate and motioned. Tate nodded his head and both men kicked their mounts into a canter. To move any faster in the churned-up soil was impossible, but the men leaned forward over the necks of their horses, encouraging them onward. The fear of what the scream meant drove them and they frantically searched the terrain ahead, hoping for a glimpse of the captor or the woman, but the crooked draw would yield nothing.

THUMBS FINALLY GOT TIRED of his pitiful game of aggravation and pushed his mount up beside the girl, kicked his foot free of the stirrup and grabbed her by the shoulder of her tunic and said, "Alright, git on up here! We ain't got all day!"

She struggled to put a foot in the stirrup as he lifted her from the ground but finally twisted around and straddled the rump of the horse, seating herself behind the cantle. Thumbs reached back and grabbed at her thigh and said, "Now, you stay right close, y'hear?" and cackled a laugh as he clamped his knees to his horse's sides to move forward. The horse was struggling as well, with the soft soil of the sandy bottom of the draw turned up like a fresh plowed farmer'sfield, each step sunk deep in the dirt and with a double load atop, the horse was working his best to make progress.

Finally, the mouth of the draw widened and the firm soil of the top of the bank gave sure footing. As they neared the edge, Thumbs saw the drop off and walked the horse along the bank, searching for an easy way to the bottom. Seeing what he judged to be an easier slope, he pointed the horse to the edge and the animal stepped over and digging his front hooves in deep and with the riders leaning well back, they soon made it to the bottom. As they started across the wide river bottom, the many bogs and marshes made the crossing difficult. When the horse began to sink past his hocks in black mud, Thumbs reached back and knocked White Fawn from her seat, causing her to land in the muddy bog. But the edge was grassy and she easily pulled herself out of the mud, to sit on the grass. She sat watching Thumbs and the horse struggle until Thumbs finally crawled off, stepping into the deep muck and stretch to the grassy knoll. The mud sucked at his feet, but he pulled himself free and once on the high ground, helped his mount from the muck, pulling on the reins to give the horse leverage and encouragement.

When the animal was free of the bog, Thumbs leaned

against the saddle, catching his breath, looked back at Fawn, sitting on the grass and growled, "C'mon!"

She slowly rose to her feet and staggered forward, exaggerating her tiredness, but waiting for an opportunity. She had already formed a bit of a plan in her mind, thinking ahead to the river they would have to cross. Seeing the woman following, Thumbs led his horse forward, carefully picking his route among the marshes and bogs and false river bottoms. He was stumbling as he moved, and Fawn knew he wasn't faking like she was, and she grinned at the thought.

CHAPTER TWENTY-SEVEN
RIVER

When they reached the river's edge, Thumbs looked at the current and knew this would not be an easy crossing. Although the bottom appeared gravelly and the water not more than four or five feet at its deepest, the current was swift and with one horse and two riders, it would be a challenge. He lifted White Fawn up and quickly followed her to mount the horse. He turned back to her and said, "I ain't gonna untie you, so if you fall off, you'll just hafta drown, cuz I cain't swim an' I ain't comin' after ya!"

He watched as she grinned at his remarks and he thought she was pleased. He didn't know that what she planned would be her best chance to escape. He couldn't see her expression but when she grunted in response to his directions, he was certain he had scared her into submission. As the horse stepped into the water's edge, the gravel scrunched and gave uncertain footing, but the heels of the rider were insistent, and the horse continued forward. As the water deepened, the current grew stronger and the horse soon lost his footing and began to bob in the water.

Fawn had pushed herself back from the man, so he could

not feel her behind him. As soon as the horse lost his footing, she slid off the rump of the animal and slipped silently into the water. She treaded water to move with the current and away from her captor.

When the horse began swimming, the weight of Thumbs made it difficult and the man began to panic, screaming like a frightened child, grasping tightly to the reins and the saddle horn with one hand, trying to hold his rifle above water with the other, but the struggling animal and the strong current forced the man from the saddle, and he was pushed by the current but he refused to let loose of the horn. His head bobbed under the surface, and he fought for air, sputtered up by pushing on the saddle seat with the butt of his rifle, each time he came to the surface, he gasped, spitting water and screamed as loud as he could, as he continued to fight for air while the horse struggled against the current toward the far bank.

Fawn had floated with the current, letting the stream carry her away from her captor. With her hands still tied together, she turned to her side, kicked with her feet and paddled with her hands, making for the shore. The wide bend of the river drove the floating woman towards the east shore, a good hundred yards downstream from where they entered the river. She kicked and struggled, was washed against a tangle of driftwood pushed against the bank by the current. Fawn fought her way onto the largest of the logs. Once seated she began working at her bonds with her teeth and using a branch of the driftwood, she soon began to feel them loosen and the blood flow increase, bringing feeling back to her hands.

THUMBS DEATH GRIP on the saddle horn paid off and the horse soon found his footing as he neared the far bank. As the horse made better progress, he pulled the man along and Thumbs sucked air that he had begun to think he would never feel again. As the horse stumbled up the bank, he dragged the man alongside until Thumbs let loose and dropped to the ground, gasping for air and happily feeling the grass beneath him. Suddenly he realized, the woman was not with him and he pushed himself up and started looking around. Not seeing her he sat up, searched for his rifle that lay between him and the now grazing horse. He stood and walked to retrieve his weapon, but knowing it was wet, he lowered the muzzle to let water pour from the end. Disgusted with himself, he dropped the rifle and began searching for any sign of the woman. He walked back to water's edge and visually searched both banks but could not see her, not knowing the bend in the river held her just out of his sight.

He sat down on the bank, thinking about his choices and chances and looked to the far bank, searching for any sign of his pursuers. He knew he had to get away, but he didn't want to leave the girl. Then he began to think she probably drowned, seeing as her hands were tied. He turned to look at his horse who appeared none the worse for wear and he stood to his feet and started for the animal. He quickly mounted, stuffed his waterlogged rifle in the wet scabbard, and gigged the mount forward to the sloping bank that would lead him away from the river. He picked a path that would take him at an angle up the sandy bank and started up without even a glance at his back trail, certain he would easily outdistance any pursuers now that his horse didn't carry an extra load.

If the terrain had allowed, the two men could have

followed the tracks of Thumbs's horse at a full gallop. With the horses digging deep in the soft soil, both pursuers and pursued had slow going. But Thumbs had a good lead and when the ravine widened to give solid footing and a view of the river, Raven wasted little time following the tracks to the slope that led to the bottom. As they crested the ridge to drop down, he reined up and surveyed the area below, he could see where the trail led into the marshy flats, and he lifted his eyes just in time to see the fleeing outlaw as he made his way up the far bank angling across the sandy slope to make his escape. Raven pointed him out to Tate, then quickly dug heels into the ribs of his horse and plunged down the slope. Tate followed close behind as Raven easily worked their way across the marshy land, avoiding the bogs by watching the trail before them. As they neared the river's edge, the men and Lobo dropped to the ground to examine the tracks showing both Fawn and Thumbs walking, then both mounting the horse to make the crossing. Raven looked at the water, judged the depth and the current and looked back at Tate, "That crossing would be hard with one horse and two riders. The horse we saw on the other bank only had one rider. Where is Fawn?"

They both looked at the river and scanned first one bank and the other as far as they could see but there was nothing. Tate said, "I'll cross over and see if there is sign of both of them. If so, you come over too and we'll go together. If not, you search the river for Fawn and I'll go after Thumbs." Raven looked at the man, considered what he suggested, and nodded agreement. Tate swung aboard, slapped the horse on the rump to signal Lobo to jump aboard and the wolf made a flat-footed leap that took him to his seat behind the cantle. Tate pushed the grulla into the water, the lead line of the black drawn tight. When the water came above his knees, Tate slipped from the saddle to float alongside, letting the grulla work the current. He watched Lobo looking at the water and then take a better stance with his front feet on the seat of the saddle and his hind feet on the rump of the horse. Lobo looked down at Tate floating alongside holding his rifle and pistol belt high above the water and opened his mouth in the wolf's equivalent of a smile at his friend. They soon made firm ground and as the horse walked up the bank, Tate strode alongside. As the grulla gained the grassy flat, Tate moved away, knowing the animal would shake off the excess water, and Lobo dropped to the ground as well.

He let the reins trail knowing the grulla would not wander off and with the black's lead line tied off to the saddle horn, both animals would be safe, but he motioned for Lobo to stay with the horses anyway. Tate walked back to water's edge, looking at the tracks left by Thumbs and his horse. As he examined all the sign, he quickly construed there was none from Fawn, indicating she didn't not come from the water here. He used exaggerated sign language to tell Raven of his findings and to tell him he was going after Thumbs. Raven agreed, indicating he would search for Fawn until Tate returned.

Tate quickly returned to his horses and mounted up, letting Lobo follow alongside at his own pace. Tate knew where the man had climbed the far bank and he gigged his grulla to the slope leaving the river bottom. He had strapped his pistol belt back on and had taken the tomahawk from the pommel, putting it back into his belt. The Bowie was secured in its scabbard at his back, and he kept the Hawken across his pommel until his rifle scabbard dried. The grulla took the slope in three easy bounds and when he crested the bank, Tate gave a quick search for any sign of a waiting ambush, but seeing none, he followed the easily seen tracks of the fleeing Thumbs.

Straight ahead was the only green showing above the

river bottom. Rising to the south was a flat desolate low plateau and to the north the prairie like flatlands that held only cactus and sagebrush. But before him was a wide arroyo with low growing green of grass and willows and alder and other shrubbery. But with a clear way between the taller brush, the trail of the fugitive was plain and easy to follow. It was easy to see the man was not concerned with covering his trail but only making a fast getaway. Tate reined up, and quickly removed the saddle from the grulla and put it on the black. The grulla had worked hard making it across the soft soil of the stampede and swimming the river, now it was time for the black to prove his mettle. He removed all the tack from the grulla, giving him the choice to stay and graze, or follow of his own accord. Tate was certain the grulla would not be left behind and as he swung aboard the black, the grulla tossed his head as if in protest, and when the black started out, the grulla ran alongside to prove he was still the better horse. Tate grinned and watched Lobo running and jumping alongside his friend, both thinking they were just out for a good run.

Tate kicked the black into a full gallop and let the long-legged animal have his head as he maneuvered through the brush in the arroyo bottom. As they ran, Tate's thoughts turned to White Fawn, knowing the reason he was on this chase was twofold. He did not want to be the one to find the body if she had drowned in the river, and his anger at Thumbs made his blood boil with hatred as he thought about what the man might have done to his White Fawn or that he might have caused her death. As his anger seethed, he slapped leather to the black, driving him faster through the brushy flats. Tall branches of willows and alders slapped at his face and he dropped his head to the neck of the black, hearing the drum of hooves as the grulla followed close behind. Suddenly they burst into the clear, the arroyo widened, and the brush thinned, and he saw a quick reflection of light on the ridge above. He reined in the black and threw himself to the ground on the far side of the horse just as he heard the boom of a rifle. The black screamed and nervously sidestepped away from the trail, nearing the brush at the side of the ravine. The grulla slid to a stop and tossed his head, turning back to the brush they just left. Tate rolled to a low cluster of kinnikinnick, knowing it wouldn't give any protection but might hide him from sight. He looked around, searching for any other cover, spotted a low depression behind a slight hump, lifted his head and made a quick running leap for the hole.

He rolled to his back, checking his Hawken, placed a new cap on the nipple and slowly pushed the muzzle above the edge of his cover. Another boom sounded, and he heard the whistle of the passing ball as it cut the brush behind him. He quickly lifted up and took aim at the last place he saw the reflection, saw the slight puff of smoke from the shot and fired just below the spot where the shot apparently came from, knowing it would just make the would-be assailant duck, but it would give Tate time to find better cover. He rose quickly and ran toward a large finger of boulders that stretched from the side of the ravine into the dry creek bottom. As he ran he thought, *You dumb greenhorn, ridin' into the open like that! You're gonna hafta be mighty lucky to get outta this alive.* He dropped to the ground behind the big boulder and began reloading. Suddenly, Lobo was at his side, having found a way to join his master without exposing himself by working through the brush. Tate patted him on the head and said, "Well howdy, partner. Glad to have your comp'ny."

Tate replaced his ramrod and lifted the Hawken to his left shoulder as he began to peer around the edge of the boulder to look for the shooter. There was no movement, but Tate saw what he thought was the top of the man's hat and he took careful aim, holding at the edge of the rock at the hat's brim. He squeezed off his shot, and watched, hoping to see movement that would give him a better idea of where Thumbs was perched. The hat sailed in the air, but nothing else moved. He turned back to Lobo, but a sudden growl warned him, and he dropped to his knees just as a lead ball ricocheted off the rock above his head and whined away. He looked up to see Thumbs charging toward him, knife in his hand and blood in his eyes and screaming for all he was worth. Tate was startled to see the fat man move so fast, but he dropped his Hawken and grabbed for his Bowie just as the big man knocked him backwards, smacking his head against the boulder. The shooting pain lanced through his head and he suddenly felt weak and black started over his eyes like a dropping curtain. He crumpled to the ground, but he heard the cackling laugh of Thumbs and felt him grabbing at his tunic, but his arms were heavy, and he couldn't see as he slid lower into the darkness.

HE WAS SURPRISED as his eyes slowly opened and light pierced his brain, the sensation of cold and wet on his face came again and again, his head throbbing as he fought to see what was happening. He felt a weight on his chest and tried to push against it had little strength, and the wet covered his face again. Finally, able to open his eyes, he saw red and thought it was his blood, but then recognized the sound of Lobo's whine and pushed back against the muzzle of the wolf as he looked around. He saw legs at his feet, stretched up and recognized the body of Thumbs, but as he looked further, he saw a mass of blood and raw meat above the collar of the man's coat, and very little of a face to recognize it as that of Thumbs. He looked at the smiling expression of Lobo, who was undoubtedly happy to see Tate awake, and saw the blood that covered the muzzle and neck of the wolf. It was easy to see what had happened. When Thumbs started after an unconscious Tate, Lobo defended his master.

Tate stood, swayed a bit and felt his head, found a sizable bump on the back and steadied himself on the rock. He dropped to one knee, not wanting to bend over, and picked up his Hawken, grabbed his hat and spoke to Lobo, "Let's go find White Fawn."

CHAPTER TWENTY-EIGHT
REUNITED

It was all he could do to remove the saddle from the black and gear up the grulla. The black had received a bullet crease across his back and rump from the first shot of Thumbs and it was too painful to carry a saddle and gear on the wound. Although not serious, it would need some care for the black to be useful again and he had proven his mettle in the recent conflict. He found Thumbs's horse and fashioned a lead with the reins, tying the leather strap to the tail of the black. With his head throbbing and still a little dizzy, Tate finally pulled the latigo tight on the buckskin and stepped into the stirrup, swung aboard and waved to Lobo to lead the way back to the river.

They returned on the same trail that had taken them through the brushy bottomed arroyo and into the ambush by Thumbs, but this time, all Tate expected to see was Little Raven and White Fawn. The thought of the woman made him catch his breath as he wasn't certain she was even alive. With no sign on this side of the river and finding Thumbs alone, there was no telling what might have happened at the river crossing. For all he knew her body could still be floating downstream or tangled among a pile of driftwood. With her hands tied, it would be difficult to swim, and Thumbs could have easily killed her in any manner of ways.

Tate shook his head to rid his mind of those thoughts, preferring instead to think of Fawn in her wedding regalia and waiting in a lodge for her man. He let a smile crease his dirty face and he dropped his head to his chest when another heavy throb beat inside his head like a war-drum. He put his hand to the back of his head, felt something wet and looked at his hand to see fresh blood. Apparently, when he first felt the knot on the back of his head, he didn't notice the blood, but it wasn't enough to be alarmed about and he wiped his hand on his pant legs and gigged the grulla to step up the pace.

When the grulla crested the edge of the riverbank, well back from the stream, Tate paused to look over the bottom-land for any sign of his friends. Seeing none, he pointed the grulla to the previous trail and crossed the tall bank on the angled trail that took them to the bottom. This side of the river had fewer marshes and bogs and he easily made it to the grassy patch of riverbank by the crossing. He dropped from the saddle, walked to the edge of the river and searched the far bank for any sign of Raven or Fawn, but there was nothing to be seen. His first thought was that they were farther back in the trees, but he shook his head, knowing they would be waiting for him, if they were there. He stood and walked a short way downstream, Lobo at his side, and as he absentmindedly ran his hand over the scruff at the wolf's neck, he looked at both sides of the river, searching for any sign. There was nothing to indicate anyone had been near the river since he crossed after Thumbs.

He turned back to the horses, checked the leads of the black and the bay of Thumbs, and mounted up. He looked down at Lobo and said, "I think it'll do you good to swim across, get rid o' that blood all o'er your face and neck." He slipped off his belt with the Colt, wrapped the belt around the forestock of the Hawken with the powder horn and possibles bag, and gigged the grulla forward. It appeared the water level was down a bit since his first crossing, but the current was still strong. As the gelding hit the deeper water, Tate slid from the saddle, holding his Hawken high, and let the grulla pull him across. Within moments, the trio of horses was stepping on the grassy bank and began shaking the water off and searching for grass. Tate wrapped his belt around his waist, secured it, checked his Hawk and Bowie, and picked up his Hawken and looked around. He saw the tracks of the appaloosa and dapple of Raven leading downriver through the brush and trees, he walked a short distance in that direction but soon returned for his animals.

He checked the load and cap of the Hawken, mounted up and held the Hawken at the ready resting across his pommel. The wolf walked slowly ahead, searching the brushy trail with every step. They had gone less than two hundred yards when Lobo let a low growl escape as he dropped to his belly. He looked quickly back at Tate and then to the trail ahead, indicating he had spotted something or someone. Tate whispered, "Easy boy, easy," and dropped to the ground, cocking the hammer and setting the triggers on the Hawken. Holding it at the ready, he quietly walked forward, following Lobo, until he could see through the brush. He recognized the horses, just as he heard a voice that said, "You are a noisy white man!"

"I was bein' noisy so you wouldn't get scared and shoot me!" Tate hollered back to Raven.

The laughter of Raven was joined by a familiar giggle that told Tate his White Fawn was there. He straightened up and walked quickly into the camp and seeing Fawn, went to her and held his arms wide as she leaned into him, face lifted to his with a wide smile. He looked at her and stood silently, drinking in every bit of her beauty and letting her nearness fill the emptiness he felt since her capture. He didn't want to let her go but she pushed away saying, "I must tend to the meat. Are you not hungry?"

"Hadn't thought about it, but, I guess I am." Lobo sat beside him, with his head cocked to the side, looking at the woman and with his eyes asked for a scrap. She laughed at the wolf and tossed him a bone from the carcass of the recently slain deer taken by Raven at river's edge. The wolf caught the bone in the air and quickly retreated to enjoy his feast.

Raven was sitting on the ground, leaning back against a big grey cottonwood log and Tate sat on the log near his friend. Raven looked at him with uplifted eyebrows, and Tate simply nodded in answer to the unspoken question. It was the way of men that fought together and knew the job of killing and did it well, when necessary. Tate had pushed his hat to the back of his head to cover the knot and now sat it on the log beside him. Fawn saw the blood on the hat and looked at his head, walked up behind him and spoke softly as she reached to examine the knot, and said, "I will wash the blood away and put a poultice on to take away the pain." Tate turned to look at her, smiled and nodded his acceptance and she quickly busied herself to prepare her ministrations.

Tate removed the saddle and tack from the grulla, dropped it to the ground near the big log, and hobbled the three horses on the grassy knoll at the edge of the clearing. When he returned to the fire, Raven motioned to the bow sticking out of the scabbard near the Hawken and asked, "It that why you are called Longbow?"

Tate looked at the bow, nodded to Raven and said, "That's right."

"I don't understand, Long Bow, is it longer than ours?" asked Raven.

Tate stood and walked to the gear, slipped the bow from beside the Hawken, bent and picked up his quiver of arrows and moved closer to Raven, who stood to examine this unusual bow. Raven's bow, if the bow nock or the end of the stave was placed on the ground, the upper end of the stave would reach about the middle of his rib cage. When he saw the longbow, standing taller than the tall white man to a height of almost six and a half feet, he said, "Aiieee, how do you shoot such a thing. It could not be done horseback!"

"Well, you're right about that, it's not a horseback weapon. But some of your people have longer bows they use from the ground, do they not?"

"Yes, yes. But that . . . " he nodded his head as he picked it up and examined it. He handed it back to Tate and watched as he strung the bow by stepping over the bottom stave hooking the nock with his other foot, then bent the top stave back and down, securing the bowstring to the top nock. He looked at Raven and said, "How 'bout takin' that piece of deer hide out yonder and hang it from a branch an' we'll shoot it." Raven picked up the scrap of hide, measuring about eighteen inches square, and walked in the direction indicated. He started to stop at a distance of about thirty yards and Tate motioned for him to go further. When at about a hundred yards, Tate hollered, "Bout there'll do!"

Raven hung the hide on a long branch and returned to the camp. He said, "You can hit that?"

"Well, let's see if I can." Tate nocked an arrow, lifted the bow, placed his right thumb to his cheek just in front of his ear, and stepped forward, pushing the bow forward.

To Raven it appeared awkward, even comical, to see the white man move in such a way to ready the bow to shoot, but he watched as the arrow was released and sped quickly on its way to pierce the hide, tearing it from the branch and carrying it another ten yards before impaling itself in the ground. White Fawn had also watched her man as he demonstrated his long bow and when the target was dropped, she looked at him with a wide grin of pride and respect. Raven looked at the man, downrange at the target, now unable to be seen, and back at Tate and nodding his head, said, "Longbow is a good name."

Raven looked at the bow and Tate could tell he was wanting to try it himself, so Tate handed the bow to him, gave him an arrow and waited. Raven lifted it up, and using his usual manner, sought to draw the bowstring back, but when he tried, he was surprised that he could barely pull the string no more than about six inches. The draw weight of a typical Indian bow is anywhere from forty to maybe fifty or sixty pounds, meaning that is the amount of pull required to draw the string back and shoot an arrow. However, the usual yew wood longbow has a draw weight of one hundred to one hundred thirty pounds, giving it a much longer range and greater accuracy. But requiring a completely different method to draw the bow to full pull, a method perfected by Tate since childhood when his father fashioned his first longbow after his study of the English weapon.

When Raven struggled, he lowered the bow and looked at the rangy white man with a new respect, believing his strength to be much greater than he appeared.

White Fawn intervened in the display when she said, "Our meat is ready, let us eat." Both men looked to the woman, smiling and anxious to partake of the meal. Tate quickly unstrung the bow and replaced it in the scabbard and joined the others at the fire, and readily accepted the willow branch and the freshly broiled deer steak. Twilight was lowering her curtain of darkness and all were looking forward to a peaceful night's rest.

FIRST LIGHT FOUND the three well on their way back to the village and Tate and Fawn rode side by side, sharing thoughts and plans for their future. She knew that Tate would take her from her people and she was alright with that, only wanting to be with this man that had filled her thoughts from the time she first saw him when he had sent her back to her people after he freed her from the two white men. Now as he talked about building a cabin and living in the mountains, she listened and reveled in the idea of this new life that was strange and exciting to her, but there was a little wistfulness that occasionally nipped at her consciousness, but she quickly dismissed those thoughts in favor of her imagined life with this man. Her thoughts were no different than young women the world over when they find themselves in love and dreaming of a new life far from the familiar.

Nor were his much different, for he had imagined a life of solitude and sharing the mountains with only his horse or other animal companion. But after seeing White Fawn, his mind had traveled the well-worn road of many previous generations, the road filled with hopes and dreams and adventure and now those dreams included another. Had someone else been listening, especially one of maturity and experience, they would smile in understanding, knowing the dreams and adventure would harbor as many surprises and heartaches as joyful fulfillment. But that was life, whether among the Indians, white men, or any other people in the far corners of the world, those are the things held in common by all of mankind.

CHAPTER TWENTY-NINE
LODGE

KIT AND WAANIBE STOOD ARM IN ARM TO GREET TATE, WHITE Fawn and Little Raven as they rode into the village. As they neared, Kit put his hand on Tate's knee and said, "I shore am glad ta' see ya' back, younker, yessir. Ya' made me feel plum bad that I din't go wit'cha, but I see ya' handled things O.K. Didja kill them varmints?"

Tate looked down at his friend as he walked alongside his mount and said, "Well, I didn't kill 'em, but they're just as dead as if I did."

Kit looked up at Tate with a confused look on his face and said, "Huh?"

Tate chuckled and said, "I'll have to explain later. How 'bout'chu? Did you an' Waanibe tie the knot?"

Kit looked back at his smiling bride and then to Tate and said, "Youbetcha!"

"Well, Fawn an' I wanna get the job done come mornin', so I guess she's gonna hafta go with the womenfolk an' I'm gonna need ta' clean up a mite myself. Oh, and by the way, the missionaries, I see they've gone. Did Sublette get them a good guide this time?"

"No, but I did. An old friend of man that sorta grew up in these mountains. He's one to be trusted so they're in good hands."

Tate nodded as he lifted his eyes and asked, "Same lodge?"

"For you, leastways for now, but come ta'morro ya'll have 'nother'n."

The trio parted, each to their own lodge and Fawn was quickly taken in hand by a group of chattering women and she was happily in their midst. Although the advice and counsel had been given during her first interlude with the women, the dress had not been completed with the final decorations nor was the remainder of her wedding paraphernalia. The women were giddy with their ideas and gossip as they busied themselves preparing one of their own.

He wasn't required to go through the sweat lodge again, but Tate willingly went to the river to wash off the dirt and grime from the past several days. When he stepped back into the tipi the same two elders that had initiated him into the sweat lodge were waiting. A new set of buckskins were laid out on a buffalo robe and the older and more wrinkled of the two elders, waved a hand in the direction of the new regalia for him to put them on. Tate readily dropped the blanket and donned the soft buckskin. As he dressed, the elders explained to him the tradition of the families exchanging gifts and how that would be different because Fawn's only family was Little Raven and the white man had no family. They spoke of the bride price he had already given to Raven and that the two sets of buckskins were part of the family gifts to him. In the morning, before the final ceremony, there should be another exchange of gifts between the two families and the elders waited to see if Tate understood and was prepared for this.

He looked at the inquisitive elders and nodded his head, telling them that he understood and was prepared. Because Carson had explained this tradition to him, he had prepared a special gift for the joining day and smiled at the thought, certain that Raven would be pleased. The elders continued speaking and sharing the traditions and beliefs of the people and Tate was a patient listener and learner. He wanted to know all he could about these people, the family of his intended, for he knew he would be spending a lot of time in their midst, and the last thing he wanted to do was to offend some long held or sacred belief. He was especially attentive when they spoke of their belief in a Creator, whom they called Be he teiht', and the balance with the Creator and the creatures of the Earth. Tate had already witnessed the great respect shown for the elders of the people and they explained about the four hills of life, child, adult, maturity, and elder, and that those that had lived on the four hills were to be respected. When the elders were finished, they waited in silence for the white man to ask any questions, but when he did not speak, they rose and left the tipi without so much as a look back at their student.

Tate sat back on the thick buffalo robe and gazed at the small fire, flames licking at the logs and holding his glassy eyed stare, and he thought about all that was said and all that had happened since he left Knuckles. The thought of the old-timer caused his mind to skip farther back to his youth and the time spent with his parents. He remembered the smile of his mother and her willingness to help anyone and everyone. The picture he held in his mind's eye was a pretty blonde-haired woman with wrinkles at the corners of her eyes and a radiant smile she shared with everyone. He saw her standing at the counter in her long gingham dress, a full apron, and her bare feet, toes curling up with her movements or humming of some familiar tune. She would turn and smile at the ragamuffin bare-footed boy that slammed the door open and announced his presence with a "Hi Mom!" and usually held out a stringer of fish, caught by hand, from the creek below the house. His freckles blended with smudges of dirt and mud, no shirt and only one strap of his bibbers holding up his britches. Dad would usually be at the table, reading or studying, flipping pages in a book, and mumbling to himself.

A heavy sigh that lifted Tate's shoulders made him lift his eyes and look around the inside of the buffalo hide tipi, and he wondered just what his folks might think of him now, here in the village of the Arapaho, in the far blue mountains his dad always dreamed about. He let a smile split his face, knowing his dad would be thrilled and his mother concerned, but if she knew White Fawn, she would probably be as happy as a lark at midday. In many ways, the two women were alike, always smiling, eager to help others, and openly affectionate. Tate looked at Lobo, lying at his side, rubbed the scruffy neck and behind his ears and said, "And if they knew I had a wolf sleepin' with me, they'd think I was plum crazy!" But his thoughts of Fawn made him lie back on the buffalo robe, and before long he was sound asleep.

The moccasined foot of Carson nudged Tate awake and the man was surprised he had slept so sound. The wolf stood beside Carson, looking at his rousing master as if the two were in agreement about the laziness of the man on this his wedding day. He had no sooner stood, run his hands through his hair and had a good stretch, when Little Raven scratched at the entry. Tate and Carson ducked through the entry and joined Raven at the fire where an older woman had already prepared a meal and after being instructed by Carson, had a pot of coffee waiting for the men. The men shared the meal with little conversation and when Raven rose, Carson motioned for Tate to follow and Kit walked behind his friend.

Raven led them to a fire circle, prepared for the occasion with several blankets spread around the circle. Raven was seated, motioned for Tate to sit to his left and Carson to his right. When they were seated, several elders completed the circle, leaving an open space beside Tate. When all was ready, the flap on the lodge was flipped aside and White Fawn stepped out and stood before the entry for just a moment. Tate sat entranced as he looked at Fawn. She wore a white buckskin dress with elbow length sleeves and fringe from the sleeves that hung almost to her knees, the yoke and hem of the dress also had fringe and each piece of fringe was adorned with white and blue beads and a tuft of blue feather at the end. Across the neckline from tip to tip of her shoulders was a pointed yoke decorated with the buglers from bull elk, and the short fringe of the yoke had large blue and white beads with small tin bells. The shoulders and hips held a starburst pattern of blue beads highlighted by quills. The slightest move was accented by the fringe and the decorations. She lifted her eyes to Tate, smiled and dropped her head as she walked to his side, showing the high-topped moccasins of the same white buckskin with identical patterns in beads on the toes and fringe up the sides. Tate didn't realize he was holding his breath until she sat beside him, and he drew in deeply, inhaling whatever she had adorned herself with. He smiled and turned back as Raven spoke to him and to everyone present, "This is to announce that White Fawn and Longbow are to be joined together this day and forever." The gathered crowd burst out in shouts and exclamations to cheer the couple in the joining.

As the hubbub settled down, two elders rose and came behind the couple and knelt, placing their hands on the two. Although Tate could not understand the language of the people, he knew these men were praying for them. They soon finished, stood and returned to their places in the circle.

Raven motioned to someone behind him and accepted a

parcel, wrapped in buckskin and handed it to Tate as he said, "This giving of gifts will be the end of the joining ceremony."

Tate nodded, accepted the gift and nodded to Carson. Kit reached behind him and brought out a smaller bundle and handed it to Raven. Tate unwrapped his parcel and was surprised to see a magnificent quiver, decorated with beads and quills, longer than most, and full of finely crafted arrows. He withdrew one, noted it was longer than the typical arrow used by the people and looked at Raven, who was smiling as he watched his friend. "I had our best man make those for your longbow," he explained.

Tate said, "I am pleased and honored that you would give such a fine gift."

Raven nodded his head and began opening his gift. When the knives were revealed, Raven slipped one from its carved scabbard, held it with both hands and examined the workmanship. The knives had been crafted by a smithy in the east who was well-known for his craftsmanship and the antler handle was separated from the blade by a wide guard and the blade was exceptionally sharp. These were knives to be used and Raven lifted his smiling face to his friend, and said, "They are a fine gift."

The feast had been prepared by all the women and they now busied themselves serving those at the circle and others gathered nearby. It was a joyous time and the people were especially happy having had two joinings within such a short time. But the celebrating soon wound down and everyone returned to their routine, knowing the village would soon be moving and there was much to be done. Tate and White Fawn started to the lodge and Carson laughed and Waanibe smiled as they told the two newly joined friends they would meet in the morning and waved at the two as they disappeared into their new home.

CHAPTER THIRTY
PARTING

Tate was amazed at the efficiency of the Arapaho people. He and White Fawn were still rubbing the sleep from their eyes as they stepped from their lodge to see most of the tipis already flat on the ground. The village hummed with the activity of man, woman, child and even the dogs, many of which were already harnessed and ready to pull the small travois of goods on the trail. The children, usually busy with games and play and never a stitch of clothing on them, were given tasks suitable to their size and eagerness. The women were bundling the furnishings of the lodge while the man fixed the travois to the horses. Tate looked to White Fawn, but she was already emptying the lodge, stacking robes and blankets, parfleches and other items aside, readying to pull down the buffalo hide cover of the tipi. Little was said, but instructions were relayed with motions and expressions and Tate was sent to fetch the horses to begin packing.

He returned astraddle the grulla and trailing the black, the bay taken from Thumbs, his second pack horse, the blaze faced bay, and White Fawn's appaloosa mare. He tethered the animals near the pile of goods assembled by Fawn and began the task of rigging all the animals for their journey. His years of practice served him well and the animals were soon standing hipshot, waiting for their trek. The bay taken from Thumbs was chosen to haul the travois and Fawn helped Tate with the securing of the tipi poles that would be used for the travois and the fashioning of the platform that would hold the hide lodge and other furnishings.

They were finishing the rigging as Carson and Waanibe rode alongside, they had agreed to ride a spell together until the parting of the ways came. Carson trailed a single pack horse, with additional parfleches behind their saddles. His plan was to meet up with others at Bent's Fort and take a load of trade goods south to Sante Fe.

The scurrying around of the people began to gain some order and many of the people were lining out as they prepared to depart the site of the rendezvous. The Arapaho were the last to leave the area, leaving behind trompled down and grazed over grass that would soon recover and leave little sign of the gathering at all. Several of the people came to White Fawn and Waanibe to say their goodbyes, giving minimal acknowledgement to the white men, but Carson and Tate were unconcerned for the people had already accepted them and that would not change. In just a short while, the people were headed northwest, apparently going over Union Pass, while Tate and company were south bound.

Tate and Carson rode together, each trailing a pack horse, followed by the women, with Waanibe leading one of Tate's pack horses and White Fawn leading the bay with the travois. They followed a trail that was new to Tate as it paralleled the New Fork of the Green River and would stay along the edge of the foothills of the Wind River range. They traveled sun-up to sun-down and made good time, although none were in a hurry to get anyplace in particular. Carson's only concern was to make Bent's Fort before snow and he had close to two months to make a four-week trip. Tate spent the time quizzing Carson about the surrounding country and had settled on a location to the north of South Pass that Kit recommended as a prime spot for a cabin. "It's plum purty country, big trees, several small lakes around, plenty of game, and best of all, it's so far off'n any path you might get lost yore own self!"

Tate grinned at the description and said, "That sounds like what I'm lookin' for, as long as I don't run into nobody else with other ideas. Seems like ev'r time I set my hopes on settlin' down somewhere, somethin' or somebody comes along and changes my plans."

"Well next time, anybody comes along, just shoo 'em on down the trail an' pay'm no mind!"

Tate chuckled at the thought and remembered his Pa's guidance and his Ma's example His Pa often said, "Whenever you have a chance to help somebody, you best be doing it, because it just might be the Good Lord sent them your way for that very reason." He knew he could never refuse to help someone, even the undeserving. The times he had shared his time and talents with others had always brought a bounty of blessings. He had made friends among many different people and learned many things from others, and the man riding beside him was one of them.

It was mid-afternoon when the flat atop South Pass showed the trail that Carson had told Tate about and the men reined up and stepped down from the horses to have a stretch and to say their goodbyes. Waanibe rode up beside Tate and handed him the lead for the pack horse, then slipped to the ground beside Kit. White Fawn joined the group and little was said, but the women embraced each one with hugs, Tate and Carson gave each other a back slapping bear hug and the group soon parted, but each one turned back to give a last wave a fill their minds and hearts with the last image of lifelong friends.

Tate and Fawn rode together, Lobo trotting alongside, and soon disappeared into the tall ponderosa that hugged the crest of the hill. The trail dropped off the edge and followed along the shoulder, twisting its way through the thickening timber. Remembering the directions given by Carson, they followed the trail as it made a twisting descent of a long thick timbered slope, crossed a small creek, and broke from the timber at the edge of a pristine lake. They reined up and sat quietly, looking at the scene before them. The lake showed deep water with shallows at the inlet that held a wide stretch of willows. The far side had an easy slope into the dark timber while the near bank held a wide sandy beach and scattered trees away from the shore. Back to the left rose the Wind River Mountains, and far away to the right or east stretched timbered hills and Tate knew beyond those hills lay the wide plains of the Wind River bottomland.

Tate looked at Fawn and she smiled knowingly and nodded her head. They slipped from their mounts and as the setting sun painted the sky behind them, they embraced on the site of their new home. As they watched Lobo running into the trees, jumping and twisting and sniffing at everything, they knew he had found his domain. And they knew this was to be their home in the mountains, this would be where their family of boys would become men and girls would become women, a family that would conquer the mountains and make a home that would last for generations.

A LOOK AT MOUNTAIN MASSACRE

BY B.N. RUNDELL

When a grief-stricken young mountain man goes to Fort William to re-supply, he runs smack into a bully and a drunkard. That meeting leads Tate Saint to take on the responsibility of guiding a bunch of dirt-farmers across the beginnings of the Oregon Trail and to the distant Wind River mountains and South Pass. But the bully and drunkard was loathe to surrender his job as wagon scout and his planned massacre of the farmers to plunder their wagons and sell the women to the Indians. What follows is a chase by the man mountain and his cronies and his recruited band of renegade Indians. That race would cross the wide wild country of the uncharted territory that would later become Wyoming.

But a savvy young mountain man would not be deterred and was bound to match wits and courage with these conspirators as he led the wagon train of farmer families. With everything and almost everyone against them, the people were determined to make it to the western lands of promise and build a new home. Their courage and fortitude, nurtured by Tate, would prove to serve them well as they fought off the forces of nature and the evil hordes and learned the ways of the wilderness as taught by a young mountain man that became their best friend and deliverer.

AVAILABLE JULY 2018 FROM B.N. RUNDELL AND WOLFPACK PUBLISHING

THANK YOU

Thank you for taking the time to read *Wilderness Wanderin'*. If you enjoyed it, please consider telling your friends or posting a short review. Word of mouth is an author's best friend and much appreciated.

Thank you.

B.N. Rundell

ABOUT THE AUTHOR

Born and raised in Colorado into a family of ranchers and cowboys, B.N. Rundell is the youngest of seven sons. Juggling bull riding, skiing, and high school, graduation was a launching pad for a hitch in the Army Paratroopers. After the army, he finished his college education in Springfield, MO, and together with his wife and growing family, entered the ministry as a Baptist preacher.

Together, B.N. and Dawn raised four girls that are now married and have made them proud grandparents. With many years as a successful pastor and educator, he retired from the ministry and followed in the footsteps of his entrepreneurial father and started a successful insurance agency, which is now in the hands of his trusted nephew. He has also been a successful audiobook narrator and has recorded many books for several award-winning authors. Now finally realizing his life-long dream, B.N. has turned his efforts to writing a variety of books, from children's picture books and young adult adventure books, to the historical fiction and western genres

https://wolfpackpublishing.com/b-n-rundell/

Printed in Great Britain
by Amazon

26759063R00130